RIGHT GUY, WRONG TIME

Right Guy, Wrong Time

A #MeToo Love Story

Louise MacGregor

Frayed Edge Press
Philadelphia, PA

Published by Frayed Edge Press, 2021

Originally published as *Rape Jokes* by Frayed Edge Press, 2019

Frayed Edge Press
PO Box 13465
Philadelphia, PA 19101

http://frayededgepress.com

Publishers Cataloging-in-Publication Data

Names: MacGregor, Louise.
Title: Right guy, wrong time : a #metoo love story / Louise MacGregor.
Description: Philadelphia, PA : Frayed Edge Press, 2021. | "Originally published
    as Rape Jokes by Frayed Edge Press, 2019." | Summary: Edie has an almost-
    perfect life but, after experiencing date rape, her world is changed forever.
    Then when the perfect guy turns up at the worst possible time, Edie has to
    figure out what romance and sex mean to her in this new reality.
Identifiers: LCCN 2020945773 | ISBN 9781642510256 (softcover) | ISBN
    9781642510263 (ebook)
Subjects: LCSH: Friendship--Fiction. | Man-woman relationships--Fiction. |
    Rape--Fiction. | BISAC: FICTION / Romance / Erotica. | FICTION /
    Romance / New Adult. | FICTION / Women.
Classification: LCC PR6113.A247 R54 2021 | DDC 823/.3--dc23
LC record available at https://lccn.loc.gov/2020945773

To Kevin

"WAIT, WHAT THE FUCK?"

Irina had held her hand in the air, fingers spread, to silence me. I closed my mouth, reached for my coffee, and frowned at her.

"What's wrong?"

"Tell me it again," she said, shaking her head. "I must be missing something."

"What, the whole…?"

"The whole thing," she nodded. Tucking a loose strand of dark hair back behind her ear, she eyed me from across the table.

I took a deep breath. I had never been very good at talking about sex, turning borderline puritanical when it came up in conversations with my friends. But I forced my mind back to Saturday night, the end of my date with Kieran. He had invited me back to his place, his hand on the small of my back as he guided me up the stairs, and had poured me a glass of wine once we got inside. I had had a few glasses of wine with dinner and my stomach was flip-flopping back and forth, partly due to the alcohol sloshing around my system and partly because I wasn't totally sure that I should have agreed to come back with Kieran. But I accepted the glass, hoping that it would push me to that sweet spot where I'd had enough to drink that I stopped noticing that I'd had too much to drink.

He closed the kitchen door behind me as soon as I'd followed him in to take my wine, and then placed his hands against the door, on each side of my head. He grinned at me widely.

"So," he said, raising his eyebrows at me expectantly.

I slid my eyes back and forth, to each of his hands, and then back to his face. It felt like a move plucked straight from a romantic comedy, where the try-hard guy finally wins the girl with the newfound confidence he's earned from starting his ukulele cover band or some shit. Except I wasn't particularly feeling this.

"So," I replied, and he leaned in to kiss me. It wasn't the first time we'd made out—we'd been out on a few dates before this one and we'd shared a few kisses before that night, mainly outside the bars that he always wanted to take me to. I liked him well enough, but I was still in that fifty-fifty place where I wasn't sure if I wanted to make things serious or even exclusive yet. He was funny and clever, but he could be kind of an ass and I didn't like the thought of committing myself to someone I didn't think was actually a nice guy. I wasn't sure how he saw me, but he'd spent that evening trying to coax me back to his place and eventually I'd just accepted that it would have seemed rude not to and gave in.

We kissed for a little bit and he left his hands on the door, to the sides of my head but not touching me. I remembered distinctly the smell of his aftershave, the warm richness of it that tipped over just a touch into too much, catching at the back of my throat. Eventually, he pulled back, and I noticed that his breath was coming harder than before.

"God, I want to fuck you," he murmured, and the line was so cheesy that I found myself supressing a giggle. Okay, well, if that kiss combined with those glasses of wine weren't enough to get me in the mood to fall for his attempts at seduction, I guessed I had my answer as to what I wanted to do next. The glass of wine was clammy in my hand.

"I think I should probably go," I said, shaking my head and attempting to duck out from beneath his arm, but he kept it firm. He leaned in to kiss my neck and I stood there awkwardly, not quite sure what to do about it. His stubble was scratchy on my skin and I noticed that he had a bunch of plates stacked up in the sink. They looked as though they'd been building up for a month.

"I don't want to—"

"Can't I change your mind?" His voice was still low and his hands were unmoving and I shifted my weight from foot to foot uncomfortably in front of him. I needed to go to the bathroom, then call a cab or Uber and get home. It was late and I was tired and I wanted to get a jump on this hangover with a litre of water and a multivitamin before I went to bed.

"No, really," I replied firmly, twisting my body away from his, "I want to—"

His hands suddenly snapped to my sides and he held me tight, pulling me against him. I could feel his hard-on through his jeans, and I closed my mouth. I didn't know what else I could say. My feet felt as though they had been laced to the floor.

He pressed his mouth against mine once more, prying my lips apart with his tongue, and his hand was finding its way up my thigh. My muscles tensed, and I found all the thoughts that had been flooding my brain—the pressing need in my bladder, the cab number I was going to call, the idle wondering about whether the takeout next to my place would still be open when I got home—seemed to vanish at once.

He turned me around, pressing me against the door—I flattened my hands in front of me, knuckles white where they were pressed up against the wood. He pushed my skirt up—*why the hell did you wear a skirt, if you'd just worn pants, you could have*—and my mind seemed to glitch a couple of steps because the next thing I could recall was the feeling of him inside me. A numb frigidity froze me, but in my head I felt white-hot, like I was trying to claw my way out of my skin from the inside out.

Even remembering it in that coffee shop, surrounded by people and with Irina's sharp blue eyes taking me in, my stomach curdled and some part of my brain shut off, a door slamming closed before I could peer through it. I realized I had trailed off halfway through a sentence, and blinked twice to bring myself out of that night and into the moment.

"So that's why you didn't use protection?" She cocked an eyebrow at me, and I shrugged. I still didn't know what she was getting at.

"Yeah, I guess," I sighed. "I'm going into the clinic on Monday when I get…"

"Edie," she cut me off. She looked at me, searching. Her gaze flashed with something I couldn't put my finger on.

"Edie."

"What is it?" I asked, shifting in my seat, irritated. Irina's brain had a habit of moving a dozen times faster than mine did, and sometimes it was as though she couldn't conceive of me being that far behind.

"You never don't use protection," she pointed out, and I flushed, feeling dumb.

"I know, it was stupid," I conceded, running my finger along the rim of my coffee cup. She was right. Ever since my very first time, I'd always used protection. I didn't like condoms, but I sure as hell wasn't getting pregnant.

"No, no," she waved her hand, her voice somewhere between frustration and nervousness, like something was teetering. "Listen to what you're saying."

"What am I saying?"

"You told him you wanted to go and said 'no' when he tried to change your mind." She spoke slowly, not breaking my gaze. "And then he had sex with you anyway."

I stared at her for a long, long moment. This wasn't the kind of conversation that you had at eleven on a Sunday morning, in the hour or so before your friend headed to work and you went to get groceries for the week and cook something you could batch-freeze for after the trips to the gym you were definitely going to make over the next few days. The word hung in my head, the word that neither of us could give shape to, heavy with meaning. I remembered vividly how I'd felt in the moment he'd entered me—the hyperactive lethargy that pumped through my veins, as though I wanted to break free from my own skin but couldn't move a muscle. I didn't come. I wasn't even sure he had.

"Are you okay?" Irina reached across the table to touch her hand to mine, her brow furrowing with concern. I nodded, then shook my head. My throat felt freshly tarred, sticky and full, and I knew if I opened my mouth now I would burst into tears. I hated crying in front of people. I swallowed heavily—Irina must have made some kind of mistake. I must have told the story wrong. It couldn't be that. It *couldn't be that.*

"I should get going." I got to my feet suddenly, and she joined me, looking into my eyes intently, trying to read my expression.

"Are you sure you're alright?" she demanded. I nodded and scrambled for my bag, clattering over the chair as I did. I grabbed for it and placed it upright once more, trying to ignore the glances of the other diners around us.

"I just need to get some sleep, that's all," I assured her. "I'm tired. Really."

"You know I'm going to call you later about this," she warned. My shoulders sagged. I knew that if I was in her position, I would have packed my bag and moved all my stuff into her apartment and started a course in psychotherapy until I was satisfied I could help her through this, but the thought of talking about any of this ever again, even with her, made me want to dump my phone in the trash on the way home.

"I can call off work," she went on, reaching out for my hand. "I don't need to go in today."

"Really, it's cool." I waved my hand away from her grasp, my voice sounding a little too high-pitched, like someone had tightened the bolts on me somehow. She paused for a moment and stared at me, planting her hands on her hips. She was trying to come up with some way that she could convince me to let her help; Irina had always been clinically helpful, and here she had been handed a full-blown crisis to get involved with. But clouds were swimming in front of my eyes threateningly and cool sweat had sprung onto my brow and I was pretty sure I knew what was coming next. When I was a kid, I had stood up in front of class to give a presentation on the Pyramids, and had been so shit-scared that those same clouds appeared in the corners of my vision and I fainted and woke up lying in the teacher's lap having puked all over the floor in a panic. Suddenly, I was consumed with the terrifying notion that I was going to do the same thing again in the middle of this coffee shop, in front of everybody, and that this time I wouldn't have the excuse of being an adorable little kid to get away with it. I planted my hand on the table, the cool wood soothing me just enough for me to take a deep breath and continue speaking.

"I need to get back home." I looked up at her. Her eyes were filled with concern and I could tell that she would have barricaded that entire place and given me a guerrilla therapy session there and then if she thought it would help.

"I'm going to call you when I'm off work," she frowned. "You want me to call the others? Ask them to stop in and see you?"

I was stuck in what felt like an endless loop of concern directed at me and I had no idea how I could get out of it. It all felt so surreal. I had seen movies where women had— where that had happened to them—and they went home and showered in their clothes and rocked back and forth holding themselves and spent the rest of their lives never getting over it. It didn't all unfold in a coffee shop across the street from their apartments as they tried to avoid even thinking of the word, as though giving it voice might bring it to life, like those dumb games I played as a kid where I chanted the name of some supposed demon monster killer into the mirror and dived back into my bedroom before it could pounce out and kill me. That feeling, or some vestige of it, was thrumming around in my head again right then, that icy-cold fear that if I let it see me, if I let it settle in, then it would become real.

"No, don't," I replied, more sharply than I had intended. I closed my eyes and squeezed the back of the chair, focusing every inch of tension into my knuckles. They felt as though they were about to burst out of my skin. I was reminded of them against that wood in his apartment and another flash of panic scorched through me again.

"I need to go," I repeated, avoiding her gaze, sliding my eyes down and focusing in on the simple braided bracelet nestled amongst the stacks of jewelery that adorned her wrist. I had given it to her years ago, when we had finished college and I had moved to another city and spent too much of my money on getting an apartment to afford anything more expensive for her birthday. She had put it on that day and not taken it off since, and suddenly the enormity of that gesture overwhelmed me. The fact that she was here, staring at me expectantly, letting me know that she would have done anything to fix what had happened if she could—I couldn't deal with it. It was fucking ridiculous, to be running away from the one person who knew what I was going through and who was offering to help me through it, but it made perfect sense in that moment.

I turned on my heel and walked out of there, knowing that if I stayed a moment longer I couldn't be held responsible for what happened next.

I felt a shiver of embarrassment that I had left her alone in the coffee shop like that, but I knew that staying would have made things worse. I could text her later and apologize and put it down to food poisoning or some shit like that. Or, you know, I could just tell her the damned truth and admit that I felt like someone had kicked over a bucket in my head and spilled a bunch of shit I never wanted to have to clean up.

As soon as I was outside, I shot straight to my apartment. I knew that I was meant to lean over and heave a big sigh and realize without a shadow of a doubt that my life had changed beyond recognition. I had seen enough of these stories to know what I was meant to do. But I refused to let the word settle in, letting it linger uncomfortably on the surface of my brain, focusing instead on my footsteps, the feel of my shoe rubbing against the back of my left foot, the idle thought that it would cause a blister and that I really needed to start wearing thicker socks with these boots. I gripped my keys in my hand, feeling them pinch into my skin, and carefully placed one into the door once I arrived outside it. Every motion was careful and considered and designed to keep me from thinking. And as soon as I was through the door to my apartment, I sat down on the edge of my couch, pressed my fingertips together, and tried to figure out what the fuck had just happened.

Chapter One

THE NEXT FEW DAYS COULD HAVE PASSED FOR NORMAL, if you were looking from the outside in. From the inside out, I felt as though I was putting out wildfires everywhere I turned.

I went to work, I cooked dinner, I even made it to the gym three days in a row just like I'd wanted to, watching myself in the big mirrors opposite the treadmills and feeling curiously removed from the face looking back at me. I cleaned my apartment and annoyed my cat Max and did my best to ignore the texts I'd received from Irina in the time since I'd last seen her. I knew I couldn't avoid her forever, but all I needed then was space to think. To process. But more than that, more pressing than anything else, was my desire to make everything normal again, and that meant avoiding her at all costs because she was the only other person who knew what had happened that night.

I could have called my mom or something, but I had no idea what I would say to her—how would I feel if she'd been through something similar? How would I feel if she didn't believe me? How would I feel if she did? She and I had always been close but the thought of telling her that I'd been...*ruined* like that was too painful to imagine. The thought of her even doubting for a second that I was telling the truth was even harder. I was having trouble convincing myself that it had really happened—that *that* had really happened, to me—and I knew my vague grip on the truth would vanish if she didn't back me up. I could imagine her, my midwestern mother sitting there in the small kitchen that she'd all but entirely raised me in, and the thought of calling her up to dump some of the worst possible news in the world on her wasn't something I could do right now. Maybe one day. Maybe never.

I went to the clinic, came back clean, and prayed that my period would come soon so I didn't have to worry about that on top of everything else. I think the hardest part was that uneasy unknowing, the questions thrumming around my head as to what on earth I was meant to do next, or now. Should I go to the police? Call him up and demand an apology? Had it even really happened at all, or was it just some kind of misremembering on my part? I went over and over and over and *over* those ten minutes in my head, trying to find the spot where I'd said "yes" or indicated in some way that he should carry on, because it had to be in there somewhere. Because more than anything I felt this burning urge to undo what he had done, what he likely didn't even known he'd done. If I could find even a crumb of reasoning behind it, a speck of something that justified his belief that I had wanted it, then none of this would have happened and I could go on without that word, without that word describing me or him or what had happened. My period came four days later and felt like a blessing; I tried to put a tampon in and found myself still sore from what had happened. I abandoned that and bought my first pack of pads since I was sixteen.

I had these panicked little bursts of thought as my brain desperately tried to make sense of what had happened, but it wasn't until the weekend after that I was able to even say the word. I had already booked in that night with Jeannie weeks before and I wasn't going to cancel now—she'd know at once that something was up, and I didn't feel like giving her the details quite yet.

"Fuck, it's been so long since I was round here," Jeannie remarked as she looked around my apartment, stretching one arm out over the back of my couch and sighing happily. She craned her neck back to see what I was getting up to in the kitchen. "You want a hand in there, Edie?"

"No, you're good," I replied, returning with a couple of beers for us both. I tossed one in her direction and she ducked in panic before catching it out of the air.

"Shit, I thought you'd opened it for a second there," she said, placing a hand on her chest as though trying to calm her heartrate. I snorted with laughter.

"You really think I'd do that to you?"

"Yeah, I do, actually," she shot back, pushing her short red hair back from her face and gazing up at me. She had these beautiful brown eyes, revealing a softness in her that she did her best to try and hide most of the time, with her black leather and chewed-off fingernails.

Jeannie wasn't my oldest friend, but she was one of my best—we'd met when I was doing PR for the band she was a part of back when I first started my job—and as soon as I had laid eyes on her I knew for damn certain that we were going to be friends. When we were drunk, we'd recount that story as our meet-cute. Usually more than once.

I had been a little lonely after college, with all my friends moving to different cities and my small hometown feeling further away than it had ever been, and then this ridiculous, excessive woman had come crashing into my life to make it all seem sepia in comparison to her. I had never been one much for having a sprawling social group, but I didn't need one whenever I was around her. She cracked her beer open and took a long swig, letting out a long sigh as she closed her eyes and sank back into the couch cushions. She looked like she belonged there.

"Well, I'll make sure to take the opportunity to drench you and potentially mutilate you next time, now I know it's on the table," I replied, flopping down on the couch next to her and letting my head fall back on the cushion. "Ah, that's good."

"Long week?"

"Yeah, sort of," I replied, evading the question. "How's things going with that girl? The one you met at the gig last month?"

"Ah, she turned out to be kind of boring once we actually got out of bed." She waved her hand, and then screwed her eyes up at me. We'd known each other long enough and well enough that she could always tell when I was keeping something from her. It's why I didn't bother most of the time.

"What's going on with you? You want to talk about it?" She asked, taking a swig of her beer. She drummed the fingers of her other hand on her knees, a habit borne from years of playing the rhythm section in a half-dozen bands across the city. It could get annoying, but I was usually able to ignore it,

"I..." I trailed off, downing a big gulp of beer to punctuate my sentence. I knew I needed to talk about it, but I didn't know that I wanted to talk about it with her. Not because I thought she would hate me or blame me or turn against me, but because...shit, because I didn't want her to see me as anything other than her best friend. Not as a victim, not as a project, not as a counselling session in progress. But I also knew, with equal certainty, that it was better to tell her now, before all of this got pent up and came pouring out of me when I couldn't control it. I looked at her, pressing my lips together, and her face switched from playful to serious in a blink.

"You don't have to tell me anything," she said. She reached across and squeezed my knee, but I shook my head. I found myself flinching away at her touch. I just…I couldn't.

Suddenly, all the thoughts that had been stinking up my head for the last week seemed to swell and shudder into life, filling up my brain so fully that my lips felt as though they were being pushed open by the weight of them. I began picking at the label on the bottle of beer in my hand, curling and uncurling my toes on the floor below us.

"I do, though," I admitted, more to myself than to her. Because I knew I had to tell her. I couldn't go on with these thoughts so heavy in my head any longer.

"It was…I was out last week with that guy Kieran, you remember him?"

"The accountant?" She wrinkled up her nose. "Yeah, I remember him. He sounded like the fucking worst."

"And…" I put my head in my hands and took a shaky breath. The air felt as though it was scratching at my throat, and I realized once again that I was on the brink of tears. I closed my eyes, looked away from her, and told her everything I'd told Irina the weekend before. But this time, it wasn't through that haze of obliviousness. This time I knew.

"Holy fucking shit," Jeannie muttered when I was done, and she ran her fingers through her hair, beer forgotten on the floor next to her. I looked down at my fingers, and remembered them suddenly flattened against the door as Kieran penetrated me, the way my fists clenched and curled as though my brain was in the process of replacing these memories with new ones before they'd even had a chance to form.

"What are you going to do?" she asked, her voice dropping to a hoarse whisper. I shook my head, swallowing back the tears. I had been doing that a lot recently—not necessarily about *it*, but about stupid things, like my mom signing texts with a kiss or the sight of two dogs curled up together on the pavement outside a bodega. Stupid shit like that. As though my body was constantly on the brink of bubbling over with emotion and just didn't quite know when to let it out.

"I have no fucking idea," I replied, laughing mirthlessly.

"Oh, Jesus Christ," she said as she rubbed her hand over her head again, looking at the floor. "Jesus *Christ.*"

I could hear her choking up and I wanted to reach out and comfort her, but something about that felt wrong.

"Don't cry, or I will," I warned, and looked up to find her face already glistening with tears.

"You should!" she exclaimed. "Or not. I don't know. Jesus fucking Christ, Edie, what the fuck are we going to do?"

"I don't know," I admitted again. "What do you think I should do?"

"I think you should tell me where this guy's apartment is so I can go over there and beat him to death with my bare hands," she replied bluntly, rage tremoring her voice, and then shook her head. "No. Sorry. This isn't about me. It's just…"

"Don't worry," I said; I picked up my beer again and drank deep from it. "There's not exactly a handbook for this kind of thing."

"I wish I could just…" She reached out her hands to me, squeezing the air in front of her fruitlessly. "I wish I could just reach into your head and pull out all this shit and take some of it for you."

"If I figure out a way, I'll let you know," I promised her, and she managed a smile.

"I'm sorry, I'm sorry." She forced herself to look back up at me. "This is about you. What can I do to help? Is there anything?"

"Honestly, just letting me talk about it is enough right now," I replied, shaking my head. "I have no fucking clue what I need to do next. It all just feels so…feels so fresh. Like it didn't really happen."

"But it did," she said as she leaned over and gripped my knee. "You were—"

She cut herself off, as though realizing that I hadn't even said the word. I jolted slightly, filling in the end of that sentence myself. I still hadn't used the word to describe what had happened to me and I had no idea how I was ever going to. So that probably meant that I should just woman up and get it over with already.

"No, it's okay," I said, nodding firmly and gripping my beer bottle so tight that I was surprised that it didn't crack between my fingers. "I was…raped. I was raped."

The word hung between us, heavier than I thought it would have. I really thought that accepting the mere concept of what had gone down in that apartment would be the hardest part, but putting a name to it seemed to yank what had happened to the front of my mind and leave it there for me to deal with, like when Max threw up on the end of the bed while I was asleep and made sure to tread it into the covers for when I woke up. My stomach twisted, the beer threatened to come back up in spectacular fashion, but I pressed my closed fist to my mouth and after a moment it settled again. Jeannie observed me with anguish in her eyes.

"Fuck, Edie." She leaned back. "I love you, you know that, right? And if you ever need anything, you know I'm here?"

"I know that," I said, nodding. "And the same goes for you. Always."

"Always," she replied, and leaned over and clinked her beer bottle against mine. Somewhere inside me I managed to muster up a smile, even though the word felt like it was pinning me down like some ancient anchor.

"Tell me about this girl," I ordered, and she frowned.

"Are you sure you don't want to…?"

"I'm sure that I've spent enough time thinking about it this week as it is," I replied firmly. "And I want to hear about the boring girl who just happened to be good in the sack. So, tell me about her."

"Well," Jeannie began shakily. "It started after the show I played at the Omicron a few days ago, right?"

"Right." I leaned back, and let her story wash over me, savouring the chance to distract myself even for a few hours. Jeannie seemed to carefully dance around the subject, never once addressing it, but leaving the door open if I needed to go back there. We drank, and I laughed at her stories from the month we'd spent apart. It felt good. And then, of course, the end of the night came and she had to leave—we were out of beer and I didn't have any excuse to keep her here.

She hugged me tight at the door, swaying slightly, and I told her to text me when she was home alright, as I always did, and watched as she climbed into the cab that was waiting for her in the street below. I went to clean up the beers that we'd put away over the course of the evening, yawning and dumping them in a tuneless clatter of glass into the recycle bin behind the kitchen door.

And then, I glanced over my shoulder and looked at the spot where she'd been sitting when I'd told her. All of a sudden, I felt my knees give out from underneath me, planting my hands on the floor as I fell, and I burst into giant, wracking sobs—the kind that seemed to unhinge me at the seams, tearing at my throat so hard they actually hurt. It was as though all the times I'd choked up over the last week had come gushing out of me at once. I hadn't cried properly in such a long time that it caught me off my guard, like a punch to the jaw—I wasn't used to it, and my face ached as my mouth gaped to encompass all the years I had held it in.

I thought it would feel cathartic, but it didn't. It hurt. Physically. I lay my head down on the thick rug on the floor. It was one that my mother had sent over from my bedroom back home when I'd gotten this place, and I bawled so hard that my stomach hurt and my lungs burned and my throat felt as though it was going to tear into pieces.

Chapter Two

AFTER THAT NIGHT, THINGS FELT DIFFERENT. Now that I had allowed myself to cry once, I felt as though I was always teetering on the brink of sobbing at any given moment. My mind wouldn't stop running through what had happened, over and over again, like a bad dream that I couldn't quite shake or an irritating song that wouldn't get out of the back of my head. But somehow, it wasn't detailed, it was still in broad strokes: the sight of his hands on either side of my head, the thick smell of his aftershave, the feel of him pushing his way inside of me, the seizing fear that seemed to still my heart and my muscles into nothing—

"Edie?"

I blinked twice. I was sitting in a conference room at work, meeting with a new band about signing them to the label. I had been working for Ebert Records for several years now and was a junior executive, which meant that I had a decent amount of sway in who we signed. The band I was sitting with, a three-piece shoegaze act from one city over, had driven in specifically to be here and the least they deserved was my actual attention. The woman who spoke, the lead singer and keyboardist, was looking at me with big, watery eyes that told me I had missed something important.

"Sorry, what was that?" I turned to the other executive who was with me, Dominic. He cocked an eyebrow at me, clearly unimpressed at my lack of attention. Dressed as he was in his dark suit, with his boring brown hair and his shapeless brown beard, I wondered how he could have been that surprised that I'd forgotten he was in the room.

"I was just telling these three about how much you loved their EP," he reminded me, and I nodded, leaning forward and clasping my hands on the table in front of me. He was eyeing me with an open dissatisfaction and I felt myself bristle in irritation. He put a certain emphasis on the *you* part of that sentence, as though he wanted to make the distinction that he didn't actually care for it very much. Like he hadn't made that clear enough already.

"I was really impressed with the production," I agreed. "But how does that translate live? Do you play with a backing track, or...?"

"Sometimes," the woman—Katie?—said. "But most of the time we just do stripped-back versions of what's on the recordings. I think that..."

She went on, and I found myself mentally checking out once more. I'd been drifting in and out of reality all week long, and I needed to do better. I forced myself to pay attention to what she was saying, trying to remember specifics I could throw in about the EP I had listened to by them. A track name? A lyric? Nothing was coming to mind. It was like everything had been shoved out of my brain but *it* and I hated the way this felt, like an enormous white wall with a single black spot on it that you couldn't pull your eyes away from.

The meeting came to an end and we swapped handshakes and promises to get back in touch soon, and the three band members filed out exchanging hopeful looks with one another as they went. I remembered what it had been like to be where they were, to have to leave my fate in the hands of somebody else. When I had applied for this job, I had been at the mercy of the higher-ups who had seemed so less than impressed during my interview. I remembered pacing up and down in my apartment until my legs ached, unable to sit still.

I wouldn't go back to that time for anything, and I knew you had to be insanely dedicated to your craft to drag yourself all the way out to be judged by somebody else. And I couldn't imagine how it would feel if the person who was meant to be paying attention to you still had one foot in last weekend. Dominic pushed the door shut behind them with a goodbye smile and then turned to me.

"What's up with you?" he demanded, planting his hands on the table. I shook my head. For once, I knew he was actually right to be pissed at me.

"I'm sorry," I managed. "I think I'm coming down with something, I'm not all here."

"You can say that again," he replied sharply. We got on well most of the time, but he didn't take any bullshit. Sometimes that required me to swallow some in order to make sure that it didn't hit the people we were meant to be working with. I could have done without being his peacemaker, but for the most part I liked working with him. I knew he meant well, but it wasn't as if I could tell him what was going on in my head that had me so distracted.

"So, what do you think of them?" I said, waving a hand at the spot where the group had just been standing, and he shrugged.

"The Tantrums? Could go either way, I think I'd need to see them perform to get a really good idea," he replied. "You want to see if they'll give you tickets to their next gig?"

"Sure," I said, pinching the bridge of my nose. I knew I couldn't drift off if I was standing in front of a stage.

"Fine," Dominic said, and I chose to ignore the edge to his voice. It wouldn't do me any good to start with him now. I mean, in theory I could have told him what was going on—it would have gotten me off the hook, that was for sure—but the very thought of sitting him down and using those words and saying those things to him and having him mouth through the motions of sympathy he wasn't equipped to express made me want to cringe into a ball and never come out.

He slammed the file on the table shut and I jumped. He seemed satisfied, and grabbed the file and stuffed it into his bag. Asshole. He had this passive-aggressive side that manifested itself in these petty acts of dominance and control that made me want to chew him out, to let him know that I wasn't intimidated by him and that *no one* was intimidated by him and—

I took a deep breath. I was just mad. It was alright to be mad. I watched Dominic leave, planted my hands on the table—this gesture had become my new go-to for when I needed to center myself, watching the knuckles pop out white beneath my skin, a reminder that there was still blood and bone pulsing in this body of mine. I drew in a deep breath and reached for my phone. I could get tickets for the show. That would keep him off my back for now.

AND THAT'S HOW I FOUND MYSELF, a week and a half later, standing outside the front of a tacky bar downtown, peering at the smokers lurking a few feet away from me and wondering just how shitty I'd feel about myself if I tried to bum a smoke off one of them. I mean, how bad could it be? Just to feel that heated smoke in my lungs again, that sizzling, crackling burn in my throat—

"Remember how phlegmy you get the morning after."

A familiar voice came from behind me, and I turned to see Irina and Jeannie, arms linked and bodies close to ward off the cold, approaching. I rolled my eyes at them, embarrassed that they could read me so obviously.

"I wasn't going to have one," I protested weakly, and Jeannie raised her eyebrows. She knew that I was about as good at quitting smoking as I was at quitting drinking, which was not fucking very.

"Yeah, yeah." She waved her hand and gave me a quick hug, then gripped my shoulders, looking at me intently. Irina touched my arm lightly, a silent assurance that she was there for me. She probably didn't want to bring it up, for fear of getting in the way of a good time. I wasn't even sure what I would have done if she'd asked about it.

"You alright?" Jeannie asked. Irina glanced away from me, shuffling her feet on the frigid sidewalk below, as though she knew what Jeannie was referencing and was at least paying lip service to giving us privacy. She had now picked up my spot looking over at the smokers with a longing glint in her eye, leaving it to Jeannie as the best friend to do the checking in. I nodded.

"I'm alright," I murmured to Jeannie in response, and then caught Irina by the arm. "Come on, Lena's waiting for us inside. I'm fucking freezing."

We ducked into the venue, the kind of place that would have been thick with smoke ten years before, when smoking indoors had still been a thing. Damn, I was pissed that I'd missed out on that: the thought of being able to light up in this place, amongst the music and the booze, even though I'd quit three years before, was honestly almost erotic to me. Lena stood on her tiptoes—standing at six feet even barefoot, she was wearing heels tonight and her head bobbed above the crowd as she waved frantically to draw our attention. We weaved our way through the crowd towards her. The place was packed, a good sign. I made a mental note to report that back to Dominic and to let him know that at the very least this band could draw a crowd.

Lena, Jeannie, and Irina greeted each other with warm hugs, and I scanned the room. I was so aware of how nearby everyone was…how *intimate* this place was. I mean, I liked that normally, but the jagged proximity of the crowd, their unpredictable movement, the way scraps of conversation and laughter burst out of it made me jump. At once, Jeannie was at my elbow, gripping my arm.

"You alright?" she asked again, her refrain for the rest of the night. I glanced over my shoulder and saw Irina and Lena at the bar, picking up drinks for us all. It was the first time the four of us had been out together in months, maybe all year, and I didn't want to be a downer on it with my personal bullshit. Especially when one of them didn't have any idea what was going on.

"I have to be," I said. I managed a wan smile in her direction, feeling sorry for myself.

"I will send you home right now if you're not careful," she teased gently. I knew she meant it.

"Hey, I got you tickets to this thing," I protested weakly, and she slid an arm around my waist. Her casual touch was usually comforting to me, but right then and there, I wanted to shove even her off of me. I fought the urge. She was trying to help.

"Yeah, now we've got what we need out of you," she pointed out playfully, "we're done with you now."

My face dropped; I knew she was joking, but that sentiment had been hot in my head over the last few days. I hadn't heard from Kieran since it had happened, and either he knew what he had done and was keeping his head down in the hopes I would forget about it, or he didn't and he'd only ever wanted me for a fuck in the first place. I wasn't sure what was worse.

"I was just kidding." Jeannie squeezed my arm, pulling me away from that bad place that my thoughts had a habit of sneaking off to recently. I blinked and nodded.

Part of me wanted to reach out to Kieran. I still had his number, having not quite built the courage up yet to delete it, like he would somehow guess and be offended by it. So it was there, and I could have easily sent him a text and asked him to call me or meet me again. I could have told him what he did to me, just to watch his face drop, to see the panic overwhelm him the way it had overwhelmed me. I didn't intend to do anything about it—it was far too late for the cops now, and I could barely say the word to myself, let alone to someone who was meant to be pressing charges—but some twisted-up, sour little side of me wanted to look in his eyes and tell him, *"You raped me."* It wouldn't fix anything, wouldn't change anything, but maybe he would feel an inch of the miles I'd had to endure over the last few weeks.

"I know, it's cool," I replied, remembering just in time that I actually needed to answer Jeannie. Lena appeared next to me and pressed a drink into my hand. I lifted it to my nose and sniffed: rum and coke. Maybe a twist of lime?

"Man, that takes me back." I managed a grin, and she raised her eyebrows at me. There had been so many nights back in college when we'd ended up devouring a bottle of rum between us and spilling our respective hearts to one another. Those kinds of nights still happened once in a while, but they were getting fewer and further between. Lena was the kind of person who swept into your life twice a year and turned the whole thing on its head, making you forget all the times she'd left your messages unread in the process.

"Come on, let's have some fun!" Irina held her glass out to us as she handed Jeannie her drink, and we clinked our glasses together. "What's this band like?"

"Uh, shoegaze indietronica," I said, pulling a face and feeling pretentious at describing them that way, even though it was the most accurate term I could think of. "So, not really the kind of band to have fun to."

"I'll try my fucking best," Lena said as she tipped her head back and smiled widely, catching the attention of at least two guys standing nearby. She had that effect on dudes. She had that effect on everyone. She had been dating her boyfriend for years now, and the two of them lived together in a gorgeous apartment that I would swoon over every time I saw pictures of it on social media. She always seemed to post the most gorgeous ones right on the mornings when I had to clean cat puke from the floor next to my bed.

I noticed one of the guys who'd turned in our direction; he was the only one without his eyes glued on Lena. He was a few inches taller than me, and had one of those pointy faces that seemed to be all sharp edges—a strong jaw, high cheekbones, a long, pointed nose—like all his features were trying to burst off his face at once. He was dressed like he hadn't purchased new clothes since five years ago, in a blue checked shirt with rolled-up sleeves and a pair of straight-legged jeans held up with a chunky brown belt. On his face were a pair of thick-framed brown glasses, Rick-Moranis-in-*Ghostbusters* style. If he'd come to me as one of my clients, I'd have told him to head to the nearest stylist and get himself a full refitting. But, standing here in this crowded club, he looked kind of cute—a little out of place, like he'd been dragged along at the last minute and hadn't expected to be going out, but cute. And he was looking right at me. He smiled, an eyebrow cocked, with a *"fancy meeting a girl like you in a place like this"* look.

I stared dumbly back at him. What was he doing hitting on me? But then I remembered that I wasn't walking around with a "damaged goods" sign plastered to my head and let my shoulders unclench. I could flirt. I could totally flirt. Provided he stayed over there, I could flirt my ass off.

"Come on, let's get to the front," Jeannie said as she grabbed for my arm. "I want to actually be able to see the band when they start."

"Yeah, you're right." I nodded, and someone stepped between me and the guy and cut off the connection. I shrugged internally. Ah, well. I needed to actually get a feel for this band, whatever they were like. If I didn't have something solid to report back to Dominic, I could just imagine the barely-restrained irritation he would regard me with when I went back to the office the next week. I didn't feel like dealing with his bad humor on top of everything else, so I sure as hell had to make certain that I paid attention here.

I held my drink aloft over the throng of people, grabbed Lena's hand to make sure I didn't lose her, and the four of us made our way to the front of the room. I leaned on the metal divider that kept the crowd from the stage and bounced up and down on my heels, inhaling that familiar smell of cheap beer and dry ice. This was what I had gotten into this business for, and it felt good to remind myself just how much I loved my job. Well, most of the time. When I didn't have to deal with passive-aggressive jerk-offs.

"Jesus, it's busy," I muttered to myself. But it was too loud for anyone else to hear me—the place was packed from wall-to-wall, so crowded that I could hardly keep an eye on all three of my friends. It was a good sign; it meant this band were actually marketing themselves well enough to fill out a good-sized venue in a city that wasn't even their own. But I could still feel something clammy clawing its way up my throat.

I took a swig of the rum and coke, hoping to wash it back down, and it took the edge off. Or at least shifted it into something else. Someone jostled me from behind, and I tightened my grip on the barrier in front of me, curling my fingers around the cool metal tight enough that my knuckles went white against my skin again.

I stared straight ahead, at the dim stage, and wondered how long they were going to make us wait. I knew that musicians weren't exactly known for their punctuality, but I was becoming more and more aware of just how many people there were in this room and how close they all were to me. I took another swig of my drink and glanced around, wondering if that guy was anywhere to be seen, but he was gone, unsurprisingly. I felt a little deflated, hoping to have someone to anchor this night on to, but turned my attention back to the stage instead.

I wasn't even sure I wanted to do anything about him, anyway, but it was nice to think that someone noticed the fact that I'd actually bothered to trim my bangs for the first time in three months and risk some liquid eyeliner for a change. He was probably looking at Lena anyway, knowing my luck, and knowing the reactions she usually got from the men around us.

I put him in the back of my mind as the band finally came out onto the stage, and a cheer warmed the room when they picked up their instruments. Jeannie tucked her arm through mine and briefly pressed her hip to my side, a little nod of affection that let me know that she was there for me. I smiled, appreciating the thought, but even having her so close was making my scalp prickle with anxiety.

The band started to play without any introduction and they were good, the warmth of their sounded spreading out to fill the corners of the room. They had a soft hipster vibe to them--matching long, pale brown hair, crisp shirts and loafers on--and their music seemed to suit that, soft and sweeping. The sound was old-fashioned in theory but modern in practice, with the fuzzy guitar cut through by the melodic keyboard work. It was almost enough to distract me. Almost.

People were dancing, and I glanced over to see Lena and Irina (a fun little rhyming couplet that I always repeated in my head after a couple of drinks, *Lena and Irina, Irina and Lena*) taking up space and throwing some shapes. A couple of guys were watching them from a few feet away, their eyes appreciatively working their way up and down my friends' bodies in a way that made my skin crawl.

They looked like they were having a good time, and I tried to muster a smile but managed only a grimace. For fuck's sake. My friends had come out, they had made this effort to support me, and here I was acting like I had stepped in dogshit in a new pair of sneakers. I was being an asshole and I needed to get over myself. I swallowed another gulp of the drink in my hand, more to dull the sharp edges of my nerves than anything else. Why was I being like this? Why couldn't I just pull myself together and relax?

Of course, I knew why. It was nagging away at the back of my head, thrumming and pulsing insistently. I didn't like all these *people* around me, so close to me, so unpredictable. Every little touch that I felt, even when it was completely unintentional and innocent, had my toes curling in my shoes. But I couldn't let this get to me. I couldn't let this stupid, shitty, fucking thing ruin my life.

Still, every time I felt someone's hand on my back as they made their way past me, or an elbow to my waist, or an accidental kick to the back of my ankle, adrenalin seared a path through my chest and I had to gulp down deep breaths to get myself back to reality. The booze was starting to churn in my stomach, but I downed the rest of the glass anyway. I knew it was a bad idea, but I didn't give a shit.

The music felt as though it was crushing me, clinging to me like plastic wrap, tightening around me till there was nothing else I could focus on. I looked down at my feet, wriggling my toes, trying to focus, but my head was swimming and I felt like I had stepped out of my body: that awful, lurching sensation tilting the world left and right and then back to center. I gasped. Fuck. *Fuck.*

Clouds were encroaching on the corners of my vision when I felt it—the hand on my ass, the tightening grip of someone who saw something they liked and decided to take it. Any other night, I might have glanced over my shoulder and shot them a dirty, scolding look, then lain in bed later and thought about all the things I'd have said to him if I hadn't been so clenched up with fear and embarrassment. His hand vanished as quickly as it appeared—and I was so sure it belonged to a guy—but the damage was done.

I felt as though I was going to scream, and for a moment I wanted to, desperately—no one would have heard me, the sound would have been carried away in the mish-mash of music and people and chatter.

I wanted to crawl out of my skin, to leave behind this stupid fucking body that seemed to do nothing but betray me, and get out of this place and not have to explain to anyone why I had gone. But Jeannie had already turned around; she was still holding my arm and half-tugged me along with her, unknowingly.

"Hey!" she yelled after a guy moving away from us. He had paused to eye us both with an unapologetic frankness that told me he really thought he'd come up with a killer opening. "Hey, asshole!" called Jeannie again, but he had disappeared into the crowd.

I yanked my arm free of her grip, the glass slipping from my hand and landing with a dull, heavy thud on the ground below me. I expected it to smash but somehow the fact that it didn't was worse; I could have leaned down, cleared it up, vanished to the bar to get help, but as it was I was stuck focusing on what had just happened instead.

I pushed through the people surrounding us, trying to shrink into myself, until I was past the coat check and past the bouncers and past the smokers that I had been eyeing so jealously and out on to the sidewalk, where I planted my hands on my thighs and bent over and gasped loudly.

One of the smokers shot me a sideways look, and another—a woman—came and approached me. She leaned down to take my hand and I snatched it back before she could make any contact with me.

"Don't touch me," I warned, the words coming out as a threat even though I knew she was only doing what I would have done in the circumstances. She held her hands up and stepped away, letting out an irritated snort. I knew how she felt.

I wasn't sure how long I was out there, but by the time Irina, Jeannie, and Lena appeared to find me, my hands were shivering and the alcohol in my stomach was churning uncomfortably as I tried to clear the fuzziness from the edges of my vision. I could still feel that guy's hand on my ass, feel his fingers digging into my flesh. Jeannie tucked her arms around me and pulled me back upright and away from a small crowd of people who had gathered to check that I was alright. I wanted to shove her off me but all I could do was slump against her, my energy completely spent by everything that had just happened. I felt as though someone had stuck a pin in me and deflated me all the way out. For the briefest moment, the guy I had noticed earlier flickered across my mind, and I hoped that he hadn't seen my dumbass little meltdown.

"Jesus fucking Christ," Lena exclaimed. "Are you okay? What happened?"

"That guy in there," said Jeannie. She stepped away from me, her hands still on my shoulders, and let me lean up against the grubby wall behind me that I knew was going to stain my jacket with gross shit. "He grabbed her ass."

Lena furrowed her brow at me, and I could practically hear the words she wanted to say: *"So what? Is that all?"* Because that's exactly what I would have thought in any other circumstance. Because this kind of crap, it happened all the time. All of us, at one point or another, had learned to shrug it off because if we had this reaction every single time this happened our lives would grind to a pathetic, useless halt and we wouldn't get anything fucking *done*. Only a few weeks ago, I would had satisfied myself with a pissed-off glance over my shoulder and chalked it up to just another jack-off who couldn't keep his hands to himself. I would have moved on with my life and forgotten the specifics; the only thing left would have been a vague, lingering feeling of shame and disappointment that I hadn't come up with a snappy response in the moment

But now, I couldn't. That man, that stupid fucking man and the feel of his hand on my ass, was enough to rip me back to that doorway, to Kieran, to—

"Okay, take a breath," Jeannie ordered, and I did as I was told without thinking. The air was stuttering in my throat and it was so ice-cold that it burned, but it was a start.

"Edie," Lena said as she took a step towards me, touching my hand lightly. Her touch was comforting; I had come down enough now that I could appreciate the effort they were all putting in, especially given how ridiculous I was being. I had just thrown a hand grenade into the middle of what was meant to be a fun night out, and they were all putting up with it.

"What happened?" Lena asked again, and she glanced between Jeannie and Irina and then back to me, brow furrowed. I realized that she was the only one who didn't know. Jeannie I had told outright, and Irina had been the one there when I had first put the pieces together. I supposed this reaction would make sense to them. I didn't know if they'd talked about it amongst themselves, or if they'd been careful to keep my secret to themselves. But it wasn't a secret. It couldn't be.

Because we all had this in common. All of us understood this feeling I was having, or some version of it. That every tiny new violation brought up an old one, raked over the stolid earth in our heads and dragged it back to the forefront once more. I looked at Jeannie, and then at Irina, and then finally to Lena, knowing that keeping this from her wasn't going to achieve anything. All that jack-off with the grabby hands in there had shown me was that I was going to need all the help I could get when it came to getting over this.

"I got..." I glanced around the group again, checking in, making sure that I was doing the right thing. Jeannie blinked once, and I knew what she was trying to tell me. I should do this. I should just get this over with.

"I got raped," I said. I averted my eyes to the ground, like I was admitting to something shameful. Lena's jaw dropped, and she clapped her hand over her mouth.

Then, to my horror, her eyes filled with tears like she'd sprung a leak.

"Lena?" I pulled myself upright, my desire to fix things for her overwhelming anything that might have been plaguing me before that moment. She bowed her head, and the tears began to drip down her face. And I knew, with a certainty that felt like the only thing I could be sure of tonight, exactly what she was crying about.

Chapter Three

MY BODY WAS HEAVY. I wanted to push him away, but I couldn't lift my hands, or my legs, or my head. My fingers scratched at the wood again, peeling away the varnish and watching it come off the door in swathes, like crusted sunburnt skin. I closed my eyes and promised myself that it would be over soon, it would be—

I opened my eyes and I was back in my bed, but there were tears leaking from my eyes and I felt as though someone had punched me hard in the stomach. Not exactly the best way to start the day, but being awake and miserable was better than being stuck in that dream for a second longer. I pulled myself upright and headed for the shower, disturbing Max, who had been sleeping on the end of my bed and lifted his head with a pissed-off expression on his face.

It had been a couple of nights since the show and I had to report back to Dominic on how the band had performed. But now I could barely remember anything that had happened that evening. Not because I had gotten drunk—even though I eventually had. But more because of everything that happened after leaving the club, that had distracted me from what had gone on there. Jeannie had made the executive decision to bring everyone back to my place, and I had to admit that she'd made the right choice. If we'd all stayed out any longer, if we'd tried to pretend that night was anything other than a total write-off, it would have only gotten worse.

Lena had taken me into the kitchen—the assigned spot for enormous and important conversations—and she had told me everything. And it had hurt. Maybe worse than anything else I had been through so far. Like me, it had been with a guy she'd been dating, but for her it was a long-term relationship. She was a teenager then, maybe sixteen, and had decided that she was going to hang on to her virginity for as long as she could.

"Maybe," she said as she shook her head, a mirthless grin flickering across her face, "because he seemed to want it so badly. It was the only thing I had over him, so I held on to it. Like a fucking idiot."

"No, no," I said, squeezing her knee. My heart lurched hearing her talk about herself like that, even though I'd said the same and worse to myself over the last few weeks. "You had every right—"

"I know," she replied, shaking her head as though dismissing the bad thoughts where they'd clung to those memories. "But…we were out drinking with some friends of ours, and I was pretty hammered, and I came home and fell asleep and when I woke up he was—"

She cut herself off before she could finish the sentence. She didn't need to. I sat there, impotent, with rage and guilt and sadness washing through me, filling my head with every emotion that I'd done so well ignoring about my own…thing. Incident. Event. The worst part of it all, worse even than the feelings in my own head had had a chance to register, was knowing what she was going through. I could see it etched on her face, the twist of her mouth as she swallowed down the lump in her throat, the rapid blinking as she fought the tears away. I wanted to crawl into her head and absorb the pain for her, add it to mine, saying *"it doesn't matter, I already have my own in there, let me take yours too, it's no trouble,"* like I was offering to put her umbrella in my handbag. I felt useless, impotent, and I knew she must be feeling the same things.

At this point, I knew we were meant to collapse sobbing into each other's arms. The camera would pan out on the cathartic moment and we would finally have found someone to share our pain with, and we would both leave the night a little lighter. But instead, we both looked at our knees, at our drinks, hiding from it. There was no relief. She was on my back now, and I was on hers, like that image of the snake eating its own tail, impossible and stupid and confused. I didn't know what to say. I didn't know what I wanted her to say. We sat there in silence for a moment, the weight of this thing we both shared bearing down on us like an oncoming eighteen-wheeler.

"We should go back," she said, nodding at the door which was separating us from Jeannie and Irina in the living room. I blinked a couple of times, back to reality.

"Yeah, I guess you're right," I sighed, getting to my feet and going to the door. Before I could get my hand on it, Lena grabbed for my arm, awkwardly pinching between her fingers the fabric of the cardigan I'd thrown on.

"Edie." She paused for a moment, swallowing heavily and reaching for her drink with her other hand. "If you need me..."

"I know, I will," I assured her, and went to the door once more. But she kept hold of my arm.

"No, I don't mean it—I don't mean it like a platitude." She shook her head, clearly irritated with either herself or me. "I mean it. Just tell me. I want to be here for you."

I looked into her eyes—I had been avoiding them all this time, too scared I might see a reflection in there of everything that I had been trying so hard to avoid in myself. And all of that was looking back at me, but it felt more like a comfort. I didn't want her to suffer the way I was, but it was some small comfort knowing that someone else had the remotest idea of what I was going through. I nodded, and pushed the door open. I didn't say anything else. I didn't need to.

Jeannie and Irina spent the rest of the night putting in a heroic effort to keep things upbeat and fun, coming up with stupid half-invented card games that went on late into the night while we demolished the bottle of rum that I had purchased months before on a "wouldn't it be nice to have actual nice booze in the house" whim. They left at two in the morning and I fell asleep on the couch, fingertips dangling on to the floor.

Max woke me up brushing against them far too early in the morning, and I got up to scrub the hangover off me and order a pizza and a coke from the place around the corner that delivered early. After that, I'd done a fine job of putting the night out of my head; the carbonated bubbles and sugar seemed to wipe the memories from my head as well as the layer of grot from my tongue. The next day, I was back at work, having binged on a series of live videos of the band and hoping like hell that it would be enough to get by Dominic when I was back at work.

I headed in to the office early, figuring that the least I could do was make sure I was in before he was. He had this weird superiority complex about getting into work early and whenever I beat him to the office it seemed to throw him off his stride. That was something I would need if I was going to convince him that I'd seen enough of this band to make a decision about them. I headed out of the house early and decided to stop to pick up a coffee on the way, letting out a huge yawn as I swayed back and forth in the line. I had gone through my morning routine so quickly that I hadn't really had time to register the fact that I hadn't got nearly enough to sleep to function for the whole day. Maybe I could snatch an hour's nap at my desk? But that would be just what Dominic needed to get one over on me, and goodness knows he was always looking for a chance to make himself look like the better option—

"Shit, sorry," I mumbled, my feet slipping on a damp patch on the floor and skidding slightly back into the ankle of the man standing behind me. I glanced around to apologize—and found myself looking at a familiar face.

The two of us stood there for a moment. I would have liked to say it was some kind of movie moment, where the sound around me dimmed and nothing in the world mattered but the look on his face or the slight furrow in his brow as he tried to place me. But it didn't. Instead, my foot slipped again and I thunked harder into his leg.

"Hey, don't take this Monday out on me," he protested mildly, cocking an eyebrow. I managed a laugh. I finally figured out where I'd seen him before—the gig, before I'd left. That geeky-looking guy with the Rick Moranis glasses. He wasn't wearing them today, but it was sure as hell him. He flicked his tongue out over his bottom lip, and my eyes flicked down to his mouth and then back to his eyes. He was cute. Cuter close up.

"You were at that gig this past weekend, right?" he asked.

"Yeah, The Tantrums," I said, nodding and managing a smile.

"Oh, thank God. I've been trying that line out all day, hoping someone might actually have gone somewhere this weekend," he replied, his hand flitting up to his face and then down again, as though he was going to push up a pair of glasses that he had only just realized he wasn't wearing.

"Well, I guess you got lucky this time." I grinned back, and then cocked my head at him, realizing that I had an opportunity here. Well, maybe two opportunities.

"Can I pick your brain about something?" I asked, and he shrugged, stuffing his hands into his pockets. He was wearing a blazer, navy-blue and carefully cut, and I wondered where he worked.

"Provided I'm not graded on anything," he said, flashing me a slightly nervous, crooked smile that I couldn't help but return. He had a sweet energy, the kind that pulled my shoulders away from my ears and got me to take a breath for a change.

"What did you think of the band?" I asked. "The one we both saw on Saturday?"

"Uh, I thought they were pretty good?" he replied, sounding unconfident in his answer. "I don't really know that much about music, to be honest. I was just there because my little brother was in the opening group."

"Hmm." I pulled a face. "Would you go see them again, do you think? If you had a choice?"

"Yeah, probably," he said. "Why do you ask?"

"It's for my job," I replied, knowing how vague I sounded. We were almost at the front of the queue and I wasn't completely sure yet that I was actually awake. This seemed like exactly the kind of weird-ass circumstance my brain would throw at me while I was asleep; as soon as my cat walked in wearing a suit and twirling his moustache, I would know for sure one way or the other.

"You make a living from getting music opinions off people who know shit about the business and hang out in coffee shops?" he asked, grinning at me, his tone playful. "How's that working out for you so far?"

"It's kind of a new venture," I replied. "Dependent on how ground-breaking your opinion turns out to be. I'll get back to you."

"I expect at least a fifty percent stake," he shot back, and glanced over his shoulder to edge up to keep his place in line. I caught the outline of his jaw, the sharpness of it under the smattering of dark stubble.

"I guess you'll need to know my name if you're signing me on to contracts," he remarked, and stuck his hand out. "Philip."

"Edie," I replied, and slipped my hand into his. As soon as our fingers touched, it was like I had stuck my wet hand against a power outlet; a jolt ran up the length of my arm, but I didn't want to pull it back. If anything, I wanted to lean forward, into him, against him, but instead I withdrew my hand and dipped it into my pocket to pull out my phone and check the time.

"Oh, shit," I muttered when the number popped up on the screen. "I should be getting out of here—"

"You're not going to get your coffee?" He glanced at the counter—there were only a couple of people in front of us, but I didn't want to push my luck.

"No, you go ahead," I stepped out of the queue to allow him to move forward. I paused for a moment; I had never been good at sealing the deal, and this was no different. What was I supposed to do, hand him my business card and slide on out of there like the business-like femme fatale that I totally was in my head? I hadn't had a business card since I was in high school and thought it was cute to print my name, pun-themed email address, and high school on to those flimsy cards that came in packs of five hundred and hand them out to everyone I knew. And I wasn't quite brazen enough to ask for his number, or to offer him mine. I stood there for a moment, shifting my weight from foot to foot.

"Good seeing you again?" I managed, the sentence coming out with an uptick that left it sounding more like a question than a statement. He nodded, a genuine smile breaking out across his face.

"You, too," he replied. "Good luck getting our business off the ground."

I took a breath, let it out, and then headed for the door, checking the time again. How had it gotten out from underneath me like that? I hurried towards the office, hoping I would get through the rest of the day without caffeine coursing through my system. But, for the time being at least, the buzz of that encounter with Philip the Exceptionally Cute would hold me over.

Chapter Four

"You really think we should give them a shot?"

Dominic eyed me with something close to incredulity, and I clenched and unclenched my fists at my sides. The last thing I needed right now was him coming at me like I was an idiot. I knew he'd been here longer, but he acted as though I was still trying to work out the buttons on my iPod sometimes.

"Yeah, I do," I nodded. We were still on the subject of The Tantrums, and I felt as though I was running up against a brick wall with him and his opinions. Fuck, if I had to listen to one more dude explain to me what good music actually was, I would tear my hair out. But it seemed like a prerequisite for getting ahead in this industry.

"They were that good?" He cocked an eyebrow. "Because I went and watched that live show on YouTube and I really didn't think they were up to much."

"Yeah, but it's never the same when you watch it online," I pointed out. "You said so last week, remember?"

That conversation had revolved around a gig he'd seen at a festival a few months prior; I had watched it streamed online, and he had been sure to point out that I couldn't grasp the full scope of the atmosphere and the passion of actually being there. I assumed he was talking about the fuckton of weed he'd claimed to have smoked before the show started, but it wasn't worth arguing with him about. Dominic's music snobbery was one of the things that had landed him this job, for better or for worse, but I thoroughly enjoyed throwing his assholery back in his face when I got the chance. His lips pressed together, irritation flitting across his brow, and he waved his hand at me.

"Trust me, I have a feel for these things," he assured me. He often found himself assuring me of things like this.

"Well, maybe next time you could come to the show with me," I replied through gritted teeth, knowing that starting an argument with him about this would only end in him sitting me down to go through his extensive record collection to prove just how diverse and intelligent his taste in music by white guys with acoustic guitars was.

Wow, I was in a mean mood in my head that day. I ran my hand over my face, looked up at Dominic, and managed to muster up a smile.

"I'm going to listen to them again," I conceded to him. "But I really think you should give them another look. They're good, and the people at the gig really seemed to like them."

"Maybe I'll take a look at their EP again," he sighed, as though he was making some enormous concession to me. "I'm going to get a coffee; do you want one?"

"No," I lied. "I'm going to get a little fresh air. I'll meet you back here in a half hour or so?"

"Sure thing," he said. He got to his feet and left, and I gave him a minute or so to get ahead of me before I went out myself. I was going to get something hot, strong, and caffeinated, but I didn't want to spend my break with him. Not when I already knew I'd have to put up with his smug explanations for the rest of the day.

Ugh. I finally made my way out into the corridor, heading for the door and on my way to the coffee shop down the street, the one that I was pretty sure Dominic didn't know existed, which worked fine for me for now.

I had worked with him for almost two years, and some days I could handle him, but if I wasn't in the best possible mood I would wind up feeling like every word was going through a meat grinder.

I left the building and inhaled a big-ass lungful of air, trying to bring to mind all those calming mantras I half-remembered from the three yoga classes I'd done at the start of the year in a rush of resolution-fuelled inspiration. They didn't do much to help.

"Edie?"

I release a big gust of air and turned to see who was speaking to me. It was a voice I half-recognised, but couldn't place—until I turned around.

"Holy shit, Benjamin," I said, managing a smile to cover up the shock at seeing him again.

Benjamin and I had dated briefly a few years previously, back when I had been working with the band he was a part of. He had ended up getting an offer to join a far more successful trio on tour and had taken it up. We had only hung out a few times before he had left, but I had liked him well enough. He had met someone on tour so we hadn't picked back up when he returned to the city, but I didn't detest him enough to pretend to be my own long-lost twin sister to escape a conversation with him.

"Funny running into you here." I cocked my head at him. He looked good—there was a reason he had been invited to tour with that band, and most of it had more to do with the way his dark hair flicked back in thick curls from his forehead than with his skills on the bass guitar. He had sharp eyes and pointed cheekbones and a wide, clear smile that deserved endorsement from four out of fives dentists.

"I didn't realize you still worked here," he said, gesturing up at the building. "Are you on your break just now?"

"Yeah, but I don't have long." I pulled a face. "How's the music going?"

"Great," he replied. "I just got back from another tour."

"Oh, how was it?"

"Amazing," he sighed, tilting his head back to look up at the sky as though he was reliving it there and then. "But, it's good to be back in the city. I'm working on a new EP, got invited in to meet with Rashida about it."

"Oh, good luck with that," I said. Rashida wouldn't fall for the languorous way he rolled up his sleeves to show off the muscles in his arms like some people would.

"We should get dinner sometime," he suggested, and I found myself freezing to the spot at the thought. We hadn't actually had sex when we were dating before, though we had fooled around some; the thought of his hands on me again made my toes curl and not in a good way.

But, as I stood there and looked at him, I reasoned that this was about the best way for me to get back on the dating horse after what happened. He wasn't an unknown factor; I knew that he was perfectly alright as a person, pre-vetted by past me as if for this very circumstance. He stood there for a moment, and I realized that I was just standing there, staring at him like an idiot.

"Yeah, sure, yeah," I burbled a couple of times, pulling my phone from my pocket and handing it to him. "Give me your number and I'll text you; we can plan something."

"It'll be good to see you again," he remarked as he typed his number in. "Maybe you can help me get reacquainted with the city." A sly smile crept up on to his face, and he flicked his gaze back up to mine suggestively.

"Amongst other things," he dropped his voice a little, and I fought the urge to giggle at his cheesiness. I guessed he had gotten used to women throwing themselves at him while touring with a semi-successful band, but he was still just the same handsome, slightly goofy-but-completely-unaware-of-it guy that I had dated a few years ago.

"Yeah, right." I nodded, arranging my face into what I hoped was an appropriately serious expression. "Anyway, good luck with your meeting. I'll see you soon?"

"See you soon," he agreed, and let his gaze linger on me for a moment before he turned to vanish into the building. I continued down the street to my coffee shop, all of the irritation that had been festering because of Dominic taking a back seat as a smile cracked over my face. Okay, so maybe this day wasn't a total bust after all.

Chapter Five

"A HOUSE PARTY?" I raised my eyebrows at Jeannie.

"Yeah, what of it?" She threw her head back, carefully unclumping the mascara that she'd just swiped onto her lashes.

"I don't think I've been to an actual house party in *years*," I said, shaking my head. "I don't even know the etiquette anymore."

"Get drunk, flirt your ass off, and help your best friend hook up with the hostess," Jeannie said as she glanced at me in the mirror. "Specific enough for you?"

"Yeah, that helps," I replied, standing up and looking at my outfit again. "Are you sure this looks alright?"

"You look great, honestly," Jeannie assured me. I twisted back and forth; the dress was tight as hell. I had gone heavy on the Indian food the night before and it felt like my stomach was bulging over the top of my panties beneath the dress.

"Stop stressing yourself," Jeannie teased me lightly. "We have to get going."

"This girl better be really hot," I grumbled. "You've dragged me out during my prime lying-in-bed-and-reading-while-eating-takeout time."

"I promise you she is," she said as she grinned that cocky, alpha-lesbian smile that I recognized all too well. "Come on, I want to walk down."

"Fine." I rolled off her bed, and the two of us started to make our way to an apartment downtown.

I usually never agreed to come out to things like this, but Jeannie had already drawn a blank from her more party-centric friends so I'd been enlisted to fill the gap. And I didn't actually mind too much. I felt as though my thoughts had been thrumming hard in my head for the last few days and I was looking forward to pouring some booze on them in an attempt to get them to shut the fuck up for just one evening.

We arrived, and Jeannie ducked off to go find the hostess. The woman holding the party was the one that Jeannie was after; she'd been pursuing her for a few weeks now, flirting online while her crush was out of town, and this was the first time the two of them would be seeing each other since she got back. I doubted Jeannie would have much trouble taking things to the next level. She never seemed to.

I glanced around the hipstery apartment, and found it about half-full with people a little older than me, all holding drinks and clustered in little social groups around the edges of the room. I took a deep breath and headed for the kitchen to get myself something to drink. The best part about being out of my early twenties, I had found, was that people actually supplied the booze for you instead of expecting you to lug a bottle of wine across the city. I poured myself a vodka and orange juice and took a long sip and closed my eyes. Mmm. Finally.

I had been texting Benjamin all week, but my heart wasn't really in it. I was pretty sure that I had Dominic to thank for that, as the two of us were still clashing over The Tantrums and what we wanted to do with them. The head of the company usually left music choices pretty much up to our discretion, so it was left to the two of us to figure out our differences and make a decision. I'd have been happy to let it go until we could hear some new music or get to see them again, but he kept bringing it up, nagging me, nipping at me. I could do without that, with everything else that was cluttering up my brain at the moment.

"Hey." I heard a voice from behind me, and turned to find a woman a few years older than me standing at the other side of the kitchen. She offered me a big, crooked grin, and I returned it with relief. Thank God someone was actually talking to me here. The last thing I wanted was to be hanging on Jeannie's arm the entire night while she tried to put the moves on her latest crush.

"Hey," I replied.

"You're Jeannie's friend, right?" she remarked, and I felt her eyes sweep up and down me. I realized that what she was looking for probably wasn't what I was offering, but having no way to say that, I just nodded.

"Yeah, I should probably go find her—"

"Oh, she's off with Reno." The woman waved a hand. "Good luck getting anything out of the two of them for the rest of the night."

"You think Reno likes her back?" I asked.

"Oh, hell yes," the woman nodded. "How do you think I know who Jeannie is? Reno's been telling me all about her for the last month, it's been infuriatingly cute."

I laughed and found myself starting to relax. If there was anything that would get my mind off the frustrating week I'd had, it was a few drinks and some conversation with some snarky lesbians.

"You want to join us?" The woman nodded toward the small group she'd emerged from, pouring herself a water from the tap and taking a sip. "Always good to have someone new around."

"Sure thing," I agreed, and the two of us headed back over to the group she'd be hanging with and she introduced me to everyone. I drank fast, and before I knew it I was cackling along at some in-depth anecdote one of the women was sharing with the group, waving her hands around and letting her drink slop dangerously back and forth in her glass. What was her name again? Lori? Erica?

I bumped into Jeannie on my way back from the bathroom—the place had started to fill up and I had somewhat forgotten that I had even come here with her at all. She caught my arm before I vanished back to the kitchen to top up my drink.

"You alright?" she asked, and I realized that I was swaying slightly on my feet. Not too badly, but enough to know that I had already had plenty to drink. But there was a pleasant blankness in my head, and I felt like I had a right to indulge in that after everything that had happened.

"I'm good, I'm *great*," I replied, glancing over at the kitchen. There wasn't much vodka left in the bottle I'd been drinking from, and I'd have to move on to something else soon enough. "How's your night going?"

"It's going really well, yeah." She glanced over her shoulder at the room she'd just emerged from, but she seemed distracted. "You sure you're alright?"

"Jeannie, I'm fine," I assured her. "You don't have anything to worry about, seriously. Go be with your new lady."

"You come find me when you want to go home, okay?" She looked at me intently. "I'll walk you back."

"Sure," I replied, even though I felt a bristle of irritation run up my spine at her trying to mother me. She didn't need to treat me like I was out of control. I'd just had a few drinks, that was all, I was hardly off the rails. And it felt good, for a change, to have numbed my senses a little. After the rape, it felt as though I had spent all my time in a hyper state of knowing and awareness, and booze seemed to be the ticket to take the edge off it for now.

Huh. I stopped in the corridor. That was the first time I'd been able to refer to it as a rape inside my own head. The word just didn't seem to have the barbed edges that it did when I was sober. That was progress. I deserved another drink for that.

I returned to the group I'd been socializing with, and they parted ways to allow me through. It felt good, just being around some new people; I had forgotten how fun it was to get drunk and gossip with people who'd have no idea of the scandals you were dropping on them because they had never met anyone involved. I vented my heart out about Dominic and work the previous week, and I received a collection of sympathetic snorts and head shakes.

"I swear, you give a dude like that the remotest amount of power and this is what he does with it," remarked one of the women, who had abandoned her glass a while ago and had been swigging red wine from the bottle for the last half hour or so. "You can be sure if this band was all dudes he'd be tripping over himself to sign them."

"You think?"

"I know," she said, nodding seriously, the conviction in her voice enough to convince me. I realized I'd repeated "convince" twice in my head, and grinned to myself. I was a little drunk. More than a little drunk. It felt good, though, and I found myself taking another sip of my drink, glancing up at the ceiling and enjoying the way the pretty chandelier light fixture popped and glimmered and blurred slightly. This was a good feeling. Why didn't I get drunk more often? Sober me would give you some bullshit about hangovers and health and not wanting to accidentally end up buying forty cigarettes when she was hammered and didn't know any better, but those weren't good reasons. I had spent the last few weeks so fucking *uptight,* so lost in all this sadness and pain and insecurity over what had happened, but now that I was here and actually having a good time for a change it all felt different. Better. Better than I'd been in a long time.

"'Scuse me," I said, stepping away from the group. I'd realized with the sudden certainty of drunkenness that I needed to get to the bathroom sooner rather than later. To my relief, it was empty when I got there, and I knelt down over the toilet and proceeded to cough my guts up. Okay, yeah, so this wasn't quite as glamorous as schmoozing with a free drink in my hand, but it happened. Nothing to beat myself up about. I finished up, got to my feet, and checked myself in the mirror; the world looped dangerously to one side and I realized that I had wrapped one leg around the other and was on the brink of decking it to the floor where I stood. I tripped, planting my foot as quickly as I could manage. I was fine. I'd just had a little too much to drink, that was all, happens to all of us every now and then, I just needed to sit down and put my forehead against the floor because it was cold down there and that was exactly what—

I had been in there for about half an hour, puking up most of what had been in my stomach; it always happened when I had vodka, but that didn't stop me drinking it when it was free and there and oh so tempting. No one came looking for me—I guessed my new friends weren't that bothered by my disappearance and Jeannie was off chatting up her new crush. I was glad for the peace. I was a grown-ass woman surrounded by even more grown-ass women and here I was crouched on a stranger's bathroom floor heaving vodka-stained junk out of my stomach for half the night. It wasn't my proudest moment. But the real nightmare started when I got back up to my feet.

I looked at myself in the mirror, and that's when it hit me. Sometimes, when I'd been drinking a lot, I would look at myself in the mirror and find that I couldn't connect to the person staring back at me from the glass; it was an oddly distant feeling, as though I was floating a few feet above my body. But this time, when I stood up once more and checked myself in the mirror to make sure what had just happened wasn't too obvious, the opposite happened to me.

It was as though every feeling that I'd done such a good job of ignoring had come rushing down on top of me all at once. If the drunk me had let me put it all to the back of my head, the *very* drunk me had punched through another barrier, one that I couldn't as easily come back from. I sucked in a sharp breath as the panic washed over me, and it was just like when the guy had grabbed my ass at that gig—the exact same feeling of helplessness and hopelessness and *fuck fuck fuck.*

I was drunk enough that I couldn't put any of these emotions in order, couldn't handle them one at a time until they made sense in my head. They exploded across my brain, sparking up into panic and anxiety and everything bad that I had ever felt about myself—guilt, shame, hate— squeezing themselves together like commuters on a busy platform. If it hadn't been for the pain from throwing up that I felt every time I sucked in a breath, I would have been certain that my throat had closed up entirely. I looked at myself in the mirror and my brain tried its hardest to fit everything I was feeling into the face that was looking back at me. All the fear, all the embarrassment, all of it—it was me, it was mine, it was part of me. I gripped the sides of the sink and felt my stomach lurch once more, but there was nothing else to bring up; I just hacked hideously for a moment, splattering saliva all over the ceramic tile. I let my head droop down, as though I could avoid myself. I was scared of looking back into the mirror again, but the feelings didn't retreat just because I wasn't staring into my own eyes. They crested and swelled within me, and finally they broke, leaving my skin prickling and my lungs searching for air.

I wasn't sure how much longer I was in there. My ears were ringing and there were grey-brown clouds clawing at the corners of my vision, and all I could do was stare at the limescale around the bottom of the hot tap on this woman's sink. I wasn't even sure if I breathed or blinked; the only thing I could focus on was forcing those feelings back into their hole, back to where they'd come from, and making sure that they never came out again.

It wasn't until I heard a knock on the door that I realized where I was—that this was the only bathroom and that I had been hogging it for the better part of an hour. I blinked, my eyes watering from being open so long, and glanced back up at myself in the mirror. This time, my face didn't hold the same spell, and the feelings retreated to some uneasy middle ground at the back of my mind. I took a deep, shaky breath, my lungs and throat still burning, and then went to the door. To my utter relief, Jeannie was standing on the other side; if someone else had seen me like this, I wasn't sure I could have lived it down. Of course that was ridiculous because I doubted if anyone else here would see me ever again, but a familiar face was the only thing that seemed to bring me back down to Earth.

Jeannie's brow furrowed as soon as she laid eyes on me, her gaze shifting down and across my body; I looked down and realized that my skirt had bunched up where I'd been kneeling down, and my sleeve was stained where I'd tried to wash my hands earlier.

"Jesus, what happened?" she asked. "Are you alright?"

I knew that the polite thing to do would have been to dismiss her and tell her that everything was fine, that she should go back to her friend and not worry one little bit about me. But I didn't have the energy to put on my game face—the mixture of booze in my system and the panic attack that had left me feeling peeled open and raw didn't leave anything else for me to pretend that I was okay.

I shook my head.

"Oh, fuck," she said. She stepped forward, and pulled me into an almost business-like hug. "Too much to drink? What do you need?"

"Is everything alright?" A voice came from behind Jeannie, and I looked over her shoulder to see Reno, the woman that she'd come here to see. A flush of humiliation worked its way up my cheeks; great, now this was a *thing*. I'd have to deal with people knowing about this little drunken meltdown. A stupid part of my brain wanted to lean forward and grab her and tell her *"it's okay, it's not because I'm drunk, it's because I'm dealing with the fact that I got raped by someone I was meant to be able to trust a few weeks ago."* Like that wouldn't make the situation more brutally awkward. I managed a laugh at the thought, and Jeannie pulled away from me.

"Are you alright?" she asked again. I managed a nod, even though I felt like someone had reached inside me and scraped out my insides.

"You don't look it," she remarked bluntly, and I laughed again. It felt like the only thing I could do. I didn't have the energy or even the liquid required for tears.

"I think I should go home," I said, and within a minute Jeannie had found my jacket and was calling me a cab. It was that part of the night when tiredness and drunkenness had a beautiful baby that caused my complete lack of ability to remember the details of what happened, just that Jeannie took me to a bedroom and sat me on a bed. I remembered the sound of her voice outside the room, of her firmly assuring everyone else that yes, I was doing fine, and no, I didn't need anyone to come in and check on me. I let my head droop to my chest, staring at my hands, embarrassed that I'd put her in this position. It wasn't fair. She had come here to have fun, but she had made the fatal mistake of actually believing that I could take care of myself and not embarrass the both of us.

The cab arrived, and Jeannie walked me down to the street below the apartment. It was cold outside, the kind of cold that felt as though it would strip the skin from your fingers, but I was only distantly aware of it.

"I'm coming home with you," Jeannie reminded me—somehow, that declaration had slipped my mind, and it wasn't until she said it again as she was climbing into the back of the cab with me that I remembered.

"No, go back upstairs," I slurred, the words crisp in my head but foggy on my lips. "I don't want to—"

"Stop being so drunk and polite," she dismissed me, and I could tell that there was no point at all in arguing with her. She leaned forward and gave the cab driver my address, and then pulled the door shut behind her. We pulled away, and I let my head drift into her lap. I couldn't even stay upright, as exhaustion was already plaguing every one of my limbs. The soft sway of the car on the road reminded me of when I was a kid and my mom would be driving me back from some after-school event in the dark and I would be so exhausted that the car would soothe me into sleep, my eyes growing heavy and my brain clearing and...

"We're here," Jeannie announced. I fumbled in my pocket for money to pay the driver, but before I could, Jeannie had taken care of it.

"No, let me—"

"Get me back tomorrow," she cut me off brusquely, helping me out of the cab and on to the street, pulling my keys from my pocket and pushing them into my hands. I managed to let myself into the building, and she followed me, walking behind me up the stairs slowly as though worried that I might keel over backwards at any minute. Finally, after what felt like a mythological journey, I found myself in my bed as Jeannie pulled my shoes off.

"You'll have to deal with the dress by yourself," she remarked, a wry smile appearing on her face, and I held my arms out to her.

"I'm sorry," I apologized. "I fucked up your night."

"Yeah, but I've fucked up plenty of yours." She sat down next to me. It was exactly the kind of response I expected from her; accepting of the fact that yeah, the two of us screwed up once in a while, but our friendship was still worth it in the end. I lay back in bed and stared at the ceiling.

"Want me to stay over?" Jeannie asked gently, and I nodded.

"No problem," she replied, and ducked into my wardrobe to grab the pyjamas she'd left there a few months earlier. She headed to the bathroom to get changed, and before she had time to come back, I had fallen into a deep but uneasy sleep.

Chapter Six

OKAY. I COULD DO THIS. I reached my finger up to the buzzer, then immediately let it drop down to my side once more. I couldn't do this.

After that night when I had gotten stupid-drunk and needed rescuing from the bathroom, Jeannie had encouraged me to go get therapy. And, considering what I had just done to her, I couldn't exactly argue with her logic.

"You really think I should?" I pulled a face at her, hoping she would back down and relieve me of my responsibility; she nodded firmly.

"I really think you should," she repeated herself again. She pushed across the table the coffee she'd gone out to pick up for me, and I inhaled deeply from the caffeinated fumes. It would be the strongest thing I put in my body for a while, I could tell that for damn sure. I let my head sink down towards the table, and laid it on my crossed arms. I let out a dramatic groan.

"You're right," I conceded. And she was. But going to therapy meant that I had to admit that there was something wrong with me, and then that involved actually doing something about it, two things I had been strongly opposed to over the last few weeks. I was hoping that if I just kept on like normal then all of this would sort of fade into the background and I could pretend that none of it had actually happened. But the more I did that, the more The Thing seemed to press itself into every interaction I had and

I couldn't go on with the rest of my life like that. It made me feel like a victim—that ugly, spiky feeling of having been violated curling around me like smoke at every turn.

And so I found a therapist not too far from me and dug into the savings I'd put away to pay for my first appointment. I was able to get one for the Friday after the stupid drinking session, and allowed myself the luxury of not once thinking about it or what I was going to say or do when I was in there. But all that meant was that when I found myself standing outside the building, finger hovering over the buzzer, all the nervousness I'd repressed came sneaking up on me at once. I tapped my feet on the ground to the beat of a song I hadn't been able to get out of my head since that morning—one by The Tantrums, as chance would have it—and wondered if anyone would notice if I just didn't go. Jeannie had a way of finding these things out, though, and I half-expected her to materialise behind me, grab my hand, and push it towards the buzzer. But I knew I couldn't rely on her to guide me every step of the way. I needed to be able to rely on myself once in a while, no matter how tough it was.

I screwed all my courage to the place where it stuck, and was about to press the buzzer when someone walked out of the building. My jaw dropped when I saw who it was.

"Philip?" I raised my eyebrows, and he came to a dead halt as the door fell shut behind him with a click.

"Holy shit, Edie, right?" He cocked his head at me, grinning widely, as though he was genuinely pleased to have run into me.

"Yeah, yeah," I nodded. "I was the one vox-popping your opinions about that band in that coffee shop."

"I hope they were useful," he said, as he tucked his hands into his pockets. He was dressed more casually this time, in jeans and a smart shirt and contacts instead of glasses, but his smile was just as endearing no matter what the outfit he had on.

"If you could come in and say it to my partner's face, that would help," I said, rolling my eyes. "He doesn't seem to believe that they were actually any good."

"I'd love to," he replied brightly. "You work for a record label or something?"

"Yeah, a record label," I nodded. "And I want to sign them but he doesn't and—"

I realized I was babbling, and already probably running a few minutes late to my appointment. Was I just using him as one more excuse to avoid going? As I looked into his eyes and felt my stomach flip and flutter, I knew I would have given him the time of day even if I hadn't been doing my best to avoid my responsibilities. He was just... pleasant. Something about being around him gave me the same feeling as when I was sitting in the office and the sun came out—the warmth pouring in through my windows, brightening corners that I hadn't noticed had gone dark.

"Sorry, I should be getting to my..." I gestured up to the building, and he stepped aside. I didn't want to tell him what I was here for, although it really wouldn't have mattered. I hardly knew him, after all. But still, I kept my mouth shut.

"Of course," he nodded, and just before I walked in, he spoke again.

"Hey, speaking of music," he said, his voice suddenly took on a slightly uneven tone, as though he was doing his best to quell his own nerves. "There's this gig on Sunday. My brother's band is playing again and he gave me a couple of tickets. Maybe you could, uh, come with me?"

I paused for a moment, and found a smile creeping on to my face. It was rare that I was faced with an honest-to-goodness asking out, one that didn't come from swiping right or social media direct messages. It was kind of charming. It was *very* charming.

But I already had a date planned for the weekend—Benjamin had made plans to take me out to dinner on Saturday, and I wasn't sure how I felt about having two dates with two different guys back-to-back. I was supposed to be taking care of myself, and I wasn't sure that involved spending my weekends hitting the town with every guy who showed an interest in me. But I didn't want to turn him down—this was three times in a row that the universe had put us in the same place at the same time, and that was enough to constitute a pattern. Who was I to argue with the universe and what it seemed to want for me?

"I'm not sure if I'm going to be free on Sunday night," I admitted. "But if you give me your number, I'll let you know?"

"Sure thing." He pulled his phone out and handed it to me. I typed in my number and passed it back to him; our fingers touched for the briefest second, and I felt that same electrical tingling I'd felt before, like a small shock was passing from his fingers to mine. Probably just the static from the phone, but another convincing little sign nonetheless. It was amazing how many there were when you went looking for them.

"I'll text you," he offered, and then stepped out of the way of the door. "Good luck with your thing."

"Yeah, thanks." I smiled back at him, and before I knew it I was through the door and on my way up to the therapist's office on the third floor. I knew I couldn't linger out there any longer without giving him a decent excuse as to why I had come there just to dawdle outside a door. So Philip's presence was already doing me some good. I felt my phone buzz in my pocket before I reached the therapist's door, and grinned to myself—I knew that was a message from him, and I promised myself that as soon as I made it all the way through this appointment I would allow myself to look at it.

I arrived where I needed to be, and read the name embossed on the brass nameplate on the door: Dr Emily Rhodes. It was a comforting name, the kind that might have belonged to my mother or one of her friends. That was the kind of name that always had fresh-baked cookies in the jar for when you came around and smelled like clean laundry every single day. That was a name I could trust. With a deep breath, I knocked on the door and then walked inside.

"Hey," I greeted Emily nervously, scuffing my foot back and forth on the scratchy blue carpet like a teenager who'd just got her period unexpectedly and had been sent along to the school nurse to pick up some free tampons. "I'm… uh, I'm Edie?"

"Edie, of course." Emily got to her feet and smiled warmly at me; she looked a little different than I'd pictured, plump around the middle and in a well-fitted, slightly crumpled maroon skirt-suit. She extended her hand and I took it, feeling as though I might drop through the floor if I let go. Was that it? Could I just leave now? Was I done?

"Good to meet you," she said, gesturing to the chair sitting opposite hers. "Please, take a seat and we can get started."

When I left the office fifty minutes later, I expected to feel lighter; after all, I'd just spilled my guts to someone I didn't know, someone who was there to help me and theoretically wouldn't judge me for all the shit I was currently spilling onto her lap. But instead, I felt the opposite. Mired down. Like I had let myself fall deeper into the swamp of bad feeling that I had been wallowing in the last few weeks.

Emily had warned me this was a possibility, that things might get worse before they got better and facing up to these kinds of problems rarely made them drop away just like that. I had hoped that I would pretty much just schlurp the thoughts from my head and drop them into hers and walk out of there feeling like a new woman, but instead I felt slightly off-kilter, like someone had shifted the world four degrees to the left and I was trying to figure out why. I made my way down the stairs feeling unsteady, and when I reached the door again I remembered the text from Philip that had buzzed in my pocket as I was walking up to my appointment. I pulled my phone from my pocket—honestly, anything to get my mind off what I had just had to sit through. I thought therapy was meant to make things easier, not harder, and yet here I was relying on texts from a guy I barely knew in the hopes of bolstering my shattered ego after what had just gone down. I felt more than a little pathetic.

"Good seeing you again," the message read. "I'd love to provide you with some more in-person music opinions if you're short."

I couldn't help but smile. He was sweet, he really was. And if I hadn't had plans to go out with Benjamin that weekend, I would totally have taken him up on his offer. I knew I could have cancelled on Benjamin—he'd been the one to skip town and leave me the last time we were dating, after all—but I knew I'd probably have to see him around work again and the thought of diving behind the nearest person-sized potted plant every time he wandered through the lobby was already exhausting me. Besides, maybe we were meant to give things another chance. He'd come back into my life the same way Philip had, after all.

I never normally paid much attention to the concept of fate, but in the last few weeks I'd found myself drawn to the idea a lot. As I made my way back down the street, the air cooling around me and the sky blackening, I wondered why that was—maybe because it meant that I couldn't have stopped what had happened if I'd tried, that it was always destined to be and there would have been no way to escape it. The thought hung in my head and I rolled my eyes at myself, irritated; I hated that I still thought this way about The Thing, because if any of my friends had come to me with the same shit I would have defended them down to the ground and made them promise me never to even think that kind of shit about themselves again. But it was different when it came to me, because I was the one who had to live with the consequences of it. I was the one who had to endlessly wonder if I could have changed things.

No. For the first time since those thoughts had started mining away at the back of my head, a tiny little voice protested them. And for a brilliant crystalline moment, it seemed so fucking obvious that they were right: he raped me, and that was it, and it was irrelevant whether I could have stopped him or not because he had been the one to do it and unless I'd reached into his head and yanked the thoughts out myself, there was never anything that I could have done to change that. It seemed so fucking obvious that I felt this bubble of frustration at myself well up in my chest—and then it popped, the moment was gone, and I was back to being sure that this was as much my doing as his, if not more. I tucked my hands into the pockets of my jacket and continued walking, doing my best not to catch the eyes of everyone around me. I just needed to get home, put my face in Max's fur, and pretend for a few hours that none of this day had happened.

But then I remembered that text from Philip again, and I managed a smile. Okay. So maybe it wasn't all bad.

Chapter Seven

"IT'S SO GOOD TO SEE YOU AGAIN." Benjamin looked me up and down, and I shifted in my heels. I needed to wear them when I was out with him, unless I wanted to be addressing his nipples all night long. I forced myself to look up into his eyes, and smiled.

"You too," I offered, but my voice was thin and reedy and unconvincing. I wasn't sure what it was, but now that I was here in front of Benjamin, things felt very different from the way they had when I had been sitting around at home painting my nails and feeling excited to go out on an actual, bonafide date for a change.

The nerves had started in the taxi, but I had done some of the breathing techniques I had been researching the last few days and started to feel better; it was just a date, and I could get out of it whenever I wanted to if I felt like it. There was nothing more to it than an evening catching up with a guy that I hadn't dated in a couple of years. Knowing Benjamin, I could sit back and let him talk at me and he wouldn't notice that I hadn't opened my mouth once the entire evening. The prospect had still been attractive during the taxi ride, but now that I was here I felt as though someone had swung a stage light in my direction and wasn't going to let me out from underneath it until I produced an anecdote they approved of.

"Come on, let's get our table," he said. He nodded toward the entrance to the restaurant he had picked for us—it had been the same one we'd gone to on our first date. I hadn't cared for it much then but had been determined not to seem picky and bitchy, so I'd told him that I loved it. I wished, in retrospect, that I had been a little bit blunter. But maybe it had improved since the last time? The thought was nice, anyway, and I was surprised he even recalled where we'd gone all those months ago.

We headed inside and Benjamin gave the host his name. He led us over to our table, which was for four people. We took our seats opposite each other, and frowned.

"Why'd they give us a table for four?" I wondered aloud. "There's plenty of two-person tables around here."

"I requested it," Benjamin grinned, and for one chilling moment I thought he was about to spring a double date on me.

"Seats for us, and for the old us," he remarked, looking at the empty chairs next to us. I bit the insides of my cheeks so I didn't laugh at what he'd just said; I'd forgotten how overly concerned he'd always been with symbolism and romance and symmetry, but it had all come flooding back to me with that one sentence.

"Right, yeah." I nodded as though it should have been obvious. I was swiftly recalling why I hadn't been that broken up when he had left. But hey, I was here now, and at least I could eke out a few decent stories to share with Jeannie when this was done with.

The waiter arrived with the menus, and I ordered a water while Benjamin got started on a beer. I didn't care that he was drinking, but even the sight of the amber liquid was enough to send my memories hurtling back to that night at Jeannie's crush's apartment when I'd made a blundering fucking idiot of myself. Yeah, not drinking was the best choice for me at the moment, no matter how boring I felt every time I turned it down.

"So, how was touring?" I asked brightly. I'm sure he had plenty of good stories from being on the road. And it felt like every question I asked him, every response he gave, was another brick in the wall that kept the conversation going long enough that I could avoid whatever it was that my brain seemed so determined to escape. I had no idea what I was so nervous about but, with a grim acceptance, I knew what it probably had something to do with. It seemed like everything these days had something to do with The Thing.

"It was amazing," he sighed, turning and staring off into space like I was a camera and he was trying to give me his best angle. "I wish I could be out on the road again already, you know? We had such a good time. I can't wait to tour with them again."

"They offered you…?"

"Not in so many words, because their bassist came back from having her baby." He shrugged and shook his head. "But, I mean, she'll probably start missing it soon and need me to step in to take over again."

"Right," I said, averting my gaze to the menu and hoping that he didn't see the involuntary quirk in my eyebrow when he said that last part. Did he really think that this woman had just gone back to performing again for show while she yearned for her baby? He knew them better than I did, but *hell*. I bristled internally at the thought. Did he think that I was just moments from ducking out of this date to go try and get myself pregnant, too? Or begging him to do it for me?

"They're working on their new album now and they offered me a chance to be a session musician for them but I didn't want to," he said with a shrug. "I'm either front-and-center or not, you know?"

"Right," I repeated myself, knowing that's all he needed to keep going. I knew it was mean, but a little voice in my head, one that I was way too polite to ever give words to, pointed out that session musician work was probably more than he could hope for from most of the people who wanted to work with him. He looked good, but his playing skills were sub-par and he struggled to perform with a pick most of the time, which wasn't exactly an attribute most people were looking for in the musicians they worked with.

"What do you think you're going to order?" I asked, as I scanned down the menu and felt that sinking feeling as I realized that there wasn't much there that I actually wanted to eat. I was craving something light and classic, but this was the kind of odd hipster joint where everything was deep-fried and slapped over avocado toast. My stomach flipped at the thought of it.

"I thought the…hummus balls, maybe?" He squinted at the menu. "Does that say hummus?"

"God knows." I shrugged, and then leaned across the table towards him, feeling this sudden rush of excitement. "Hey, do you want to get out of here?"

"Like, back to my place?" He cocked an eyebrow, and I felt my stomach turn again.

"No, not like that," I replied. I leaned back abruptly, the smell of his aftershave wrapping around me, filling my nostrils and gagging me a little. "I mean, go somewhere else. This place isn't really my style."

"I thought you said you liked it last time…?" he pointed out, a furrow appearing between his brows.

"I changed my mind," I replied with a shrug. "Come on, I'll even pay for your beer."

"Nah, I like it here," he said, shaking his head cheerfully, and returning his attention to the menu. I sat back in my seat and eyed him for a moment; he was nice enough, but it was this complete and utter obliviousness that had kept me from staying in contact with him when he went on tour. I remembered that now. Would that I had remembered it in the ten seconds before I agreed to meet him for another date.

"Fair enough," I sighed, and committed myself to sitting there for the rest of the evening; it was my penance for agreeing to come out in the first place, and at least if I had a really terrible, boring night then it would stick in my mind and I would remember next time when I found myself distracted by how cute and smiley he was when I bumped into him at the office.

The rest of the night continued about as well as the first ten minutes had. The worst part of it was that Benjamin was, compared to a lot of guys in this city, kind of a catch; he had a career that he was actively pursuing, instead of lazing around in his apartment waiting for someone to point him in the direction of a job. He had a range of interests—movies, books, games—even if none of them seemed to intersect with own my particular interests in those topics. He was handsome and pleasant and chatty, and at the same time completely self-involved and almost embarrassingly oblivious and cheesy in all the worst ways possible. I spent the entire night trying to convince myself that he wasn't that bad, that loads of women would kill to be where I was right now, as though I couldn't accept that I'd been stupid enough to come out on this date and actually expect something good to come out of it. But it didn't matter how many women would have loved to be listening to his eighth anecdote about a fangirl of that band he toured with throwing herself at him while he chivalrously declined; I didn't give a shit, and I wanted this night to be over with already.

Finally, after an excruciating main course and dessert, the meal came to an end. I had been yawning for a few minutes, laying the groundwork for when I told him that I was exhausted and needed to go home. I had a bagged green salad in my fridge, and was already planning to go at that thing with a fork and no bowl, with Max on my lap, and spend the rest of the evening scrolling through the new music tags on my social media. But, despite how dead-set I was on that plan, I still had this flutter of nervousness that I couldn't quite give a name to spinning around my head.

"Well, thanks for tonight," I smiled at Benjamin across the table after we'd split the bill; he'd offered to pay the whole thing, but I always paid my half on principal—mainly because the couple of times I'd let my dates pay, they'd been funny about me not coming home with them, and the last thing I needed was to give Benjamin any excuse to try and hustle back in the direction of his place. I tried to remember if he'd asked me one question about myself the entire night, and I couldn't bring one to mind. That said, I had spent some of the time aggressively repressing my urge to laugh when the waiter brought out my "deconstructed" mac and cheese with the cheese sauce not even stirred into the pasta shells, so maybe I'd missed some compassionate conversation from him then.

"Yeah, it's been great to catch up," he said, as he touched his knee to mine beneath the table. Without thinking, I jerked myself away. A flicker of irritation passed across his face, but he swiftly cleared it and smiled again.

"We should do this again sometime," he suggested, and I made the most noncommittal noise I could manage. I feared it sounded too much like a "Sure!" judging by the grin that spread out over his face.

"I thought about you a lot while I was away on tour," he remarked, catching my hand in his. The restaurant was busier now, busy enough that if I had snatched my hand away I could be sure that people would notice. I didn't want to embarrass him, but I wasn't sure how to get him to take the hint.

"Oh, yeah?" I remarked, raising my eyebrows like he had made a comment about the weather. He turned my palm over and began to trace his fingers over the sensitive spot at the centre of my palm, and I fought the urge to whip it away. I didn't want him to touch me, but I didn't know how to tell him to stop without hurting his feelings. And, for some reason, it was his feelings that mattered to me more than anything in that moment. He had been nothing but nice to me all evening—well, maybe not nice, but passable, pleasant, prurient. He didn't deserve for me to be mean for no reason. I would just sit through this, and…

"Come back to my place," he said suddenly, clasping my hand between his and drawing it to his lips, his hot, clammy breath on my fingers. I felt the heavy food in my stomach twist up on itself and I reached for my glass of water, chugging deeply in the hope that it would keep me from throwing up. It just curdled in my stomach, along with the wallpaper-paste cheese sauce that had seemed so hysterical earlier.

"I have to be up early tomorrow," I protested.

"Tomorrow's a Sunday," he pointed out, and he turned my palm over and for one mortifying second I thought he was going to lick my palm. I had mentioned to him once, in passing, that the spot in the middle of my palm was sensitive, and it seemed like he had committed that fact to memory and thought that he now had inside knowledge of an irresistible on-switch. But my libido had curled up and died as soon as he'd referred to Budweiser as a craft beer. I just wanted to get home already.

"I know, but I've got stuff to do," I said, pulling an apologetic face. "Really. Maybe we could do this another time or…"

"I'll split the cab with you, if you want," he offered, and there was a hint of desperation to his voice that took a further dump on any attraction that I might have had to him. Jesus, what was it about dudes like this and the assumption that attraction only lasted as long as we were on a date and that as soon as I walked away from him I would forget and never want to see him again? I mean, I never did, but it had nothing to do with that.

"Benjamin, I want to go home," I replied firmly, pulling my hand away from him in a sharp motion. I caught the eye of the waitress who was lurking over by another table, and she gave me a sympathetic wince. Fuckboys were a language that transcended words.

"I'll walk you there," he suggested, and I slapped my hand down on the table in front of me. I didn't care about the clatter of cutlery, or the looks that we got from the people at the tables around us. I was done with pandering to his pathetic little ego.

"I actually live in another city now, Benjamin, but you wouldn't know that since you haven't asked me anything about myself all night long," I lied with a snarl, knowing that this wasn't going to do me any good but revelling in the satisfaction of chewing him out nonetheless. "So unless you want to walk a hundred miles back to my place…"

"I'd walk any distance for you," he announced, and I could tell from the way he raised his voice to make sure the people around us heard that he thought that was the most sweepingly romantic thing he could have told me. I fought the urge to let out a loud groan before he'd finished talking, but instead pressed my lips together. And then, without waiting for him to embarrass either of us any further, I got to my feet and grabbed my purse.

"I'm going now," I announced, glancing around at the few people who were observing this blowout with mild amusement. I was tempted to take a bow and hand a hat around for tips, but I figured maybe now wasn't the time.

"Can I call you?" He sprang to his feet and hurried around me, trying to help me on with my jacket.

"You can try," I muttered back, shrugging him off and heading for the door. As I reached it, I couldn't keep the smile off my face; yes, it had been a crappy end to an equally crappy evening, but at least I'd managed to get out everything I wanted to say to him instead of grinning to his face and sharpening my put-downs in the privacy of the taxi on the way home. Awkwardness at work be damned; he wouldn't be coming up to me and huffing all over my hand, and I would take freedom from his insistent come-ons at any price.

Ugh. And to think I had convinced myself that this guy was worth dating, not once, but *twice*. Just how hard-up was I the first time I agreed to go out with him? Was I worried that I was going to seal up and need re-breaking in, like with my ear piercings when I was fifteen? As I made my way down the street in the direction of the taxi stand, I found some pleasure in reaming him out in my head, glancing over my shoulder a couple of times to make sure he wasn't following me. He seemed like the kind of dude who might chase me down the street after strenuously avoiding the hint; the kind of dude who'd do that with a guitar. Ugh. Even the thought was enough to make my abs hurt with the cringe.

I slipped into the back seat of the cab, gave the driver my address, and let out a long sigh, an unspoken warning that I didn't want to talk about the night I'd had so far. Now that I was alone, away from the unbeatable adrenalin hit of chewing out an asshole, the night felt less like a waste and more like a learning experience.

A few months ago, I might have gone home with him, just for the fun of it. Just because I was horny and wanted to fuck or wanted the company or just didn't want the night to be a sexless waste. But things were different now. Sex meant something different from what it had before—because the next guy I slept with would be the first one *since*. And the thought of giving that dubious honour to Benjamin felt… bad. He couldn't respect my boundaries sitting in that restaurant in front of all those people, so what was to say he'd be any better at it when we were alone? Once bitten, twice as likely to turn down the chance to hook up with guys I didn't trust one hundred percent.

I pressed my forehead to the cab window and allowed the cool glass to soothe my rushing thoughts. It didn't do much good. Everything I had been sure that I'd known about sex had been wiped clean by what had happened that night, and now I had to relearn everything from scratch. Except it wouldn't be like before, when I had been learning along with the partners I had—no, sex was a given when it came to dating, something that people just assumed you'd be able to without hang-ups. But it would never be that for me again. It would always be something. Sex now would be a way to bury the memory of that night. I would never hook up with a fuckboy like Benjamin again just for the fun of it, because the fun of it had been taken from me when someone had decided that I would be their bit of fun whether I liked it or not. Fuck. *Fuck.* Sometimes it felt unfair more than anything else, the knowledge that Kieran was just out there wandering around without knowing what he'd taken from me. I wanted to track him down and tell him everything that he'd done to me and taken from me and changed in me. But it wouldn't change anything. I couldn't pull the thoughts from my head and dump them into his. There wasn't going to be a time when this hadn't happened to me.

I pulled out my phone and checked the time, and remembered briefly walking out of that therapy appointment and what had brought me a smile then. I pulled up Philip's message and looked at it for a moment, tracing the words in my mind. Well, I had told Benjamin that I plans tomorrow.

"Hey," I texted quickly, before I had a chance to think about what I was doing. "You still going out tomorrow?"

He got back to me a minute or so later, and I bit my lip as I opened up the message. My heart swooped as I opened up his message, a stark difference to how I had felt when Benjamin was making plans with me earlier in the week.

"Need to pick my brains again? I guess I could manage one more night," the message read. "Tomorrow night at seven at the Artemis?"

"I'll see you there," I texted back quickly, and turned to look back out the window. Okay, so maybe this night hadn't been a total write-off after all.

Chapter Eight

"Relax, you're going to be fine," Jeannie assured me, and I stopped craning my neck for a moment to shoot her a look.

"Let me be insecure," I protested. "I'm only, like, twenty hours out from the worst date of my entire life."

"Oh, God, don't remind me," she rolled her eyes. "That thing with the table? And the extra seats?"

"I should have left then," I groaned, slumping back down into my seat and closing my eyes. "I could have been doing something useful that night."

"Like calling every woman in the city and warning them not to go near Benjamin?" Jeannie suggested. When she had heard that I was going out with Philip so soon after the atrocious Benjamin date, she had invited herself and her new crush, Reno, along to join us. I wasn't sure it was exactly conducive to romance, having my friend turn this into a double date with only an hour's notice, but at least I had someone I knew I'd actually enjoy hanging out with should Philip prove to be another dead end.

"I was thinking more like lying in a dark room staring at a blank ceiling for nine hours, but I like your idea better," I conceded. "When did you say you were meeting Reno?"

"She said at eight, but she's not great with time," Jeannie answered. "What about your man?"

"He's not my man," I said, shaking my head. "This is just a palette cleanser. Get the taste of last night out my mouth and remind me that not all men are complete garbage."

"I wouldn't be so sure about that," she said, nudging me with her knee beneath the table.

"I feel like you're not the most impartial person on this topic," I pointed out, and she held her hands up.

"Hey, I've dated guys," she protested.

"How many decades ago now?"

"Not the point." She picked up her drink, then put it down again. "Hey, there she is! Give me a minute, I'm just going to get her a drink and then I'll be back over."

"Sure." I waved my hand, and watched her go. We were in the bar area of the Artemis, a little hipster club a dozen blocks from my place, and it was buzzing. I couldn't say I remembered much about the band when they'd been opening for The Tantrums, but I wasn't here to work. I was here to go on a date with a guy who seemed like less of a raging shit than the last one I'd been out with. And he was already five minutes late, so not off to the best start.

"Hey, sorry I'm late, my brother needed a hand getting his shit into the venue…"

I turned and found a slightly flustered-looking Philip approaching me from behind. He was slightly damp from the rain outside, and a thick pair of glasses perched on his nose. He leaned down to plant a quick kiss on my cheek in greeting, and I blinked and smiled as he took a seat next to me.

"Forgiven," I replied. "If there's anything I know about first-hand, it's that musicians are generally the least organized people in the world."

"Are you the one doing the wrangling most of the time?" he asked, glancing around the place and settling back into his seat. I liked the expression he had on his face, like he would have been happy sitting there all night long and just taking in the world around him. I could never find that kind of chilled-out peace, no matter how much time I spent forcing myself into yoga classes.

"Most of the time," I agreed, picking up my drink. I had decided to hold off on booze that evening, just as I had done with Benjamin the night before. Alcohol seemed to make me a whole lot more tolerant of bullshit, and I had no intention of letting myself get stuck out on another date I'd regret.

"So, any advancement on that band?" He raised his eyebrows at me.

"I wish," I sighed, tilting my head back. "But trust me, I don't want to talk about work."

"I can get behind that," he grinned, and I realized that I had no idea what he even did for a living. I smiled to myself and shook my head.

"What is it?" he asked, fiddling with his glasses, pulling them off and cleaning them on the edge of his vintage band shirt.

"I just realized that I really don't know anything about you," I admitted. "I don't normally accept dates from guys I don't know anything about."

"Hey, who says this is a date?" he teased. "That's a little forward of you."

"Well, say it is," I played along. "What should I know about you?"

"Uh…" He raised his eyebrows. "Good question. How much do you want to know?"

"Let's save something for date number two," I replied, and then quickly jumped in to correct myself. "If there is one."

"Okay, pressure's on," he said as he leaned back. "I'm Philip Moore, I'm thirty but haven't accepted it yet, I work as a freelancer, mostly copywriting but some creative stuff too, I grew up in the city, moved to the country and hated it, and came back a few months ago…"

"Why did you hate the country?"

"Too far from everything," he said, shaking his head. "I convinced myself that what I needed was to get away from everything going on here, all the people and the activity and stuff, but it turned out that I need that to get by. Working from home I just didn't see anyone, and it didn't suit me. Didn't help than none of my friends want to travel much past the city boundaries so they weren't too keen to visit. It was just lonely, I guess."

"What prompted the move?" I wondered aloud. "Not the kind of thing you do if everything in your life is otherwise perfect."

"You got me," he said, holding his hands up sheepishly. "I came out of a rough break-up. Really shitty. Kind of threw me off balance for a while, I guess."

"So, you went to the country to try and get a fresh start?"

"Got the dramatic haircut as well," he replied, managing a smile. "You should have seen it. I shaved my whole head bald. I looked like Edward Norton in *American History X*."

"But less Nazism?"

"Considerably less."

"Oh, hey, you're here!" Jeannie appeared over his shoulder with Reno in tow, and Philip turned to see who was there.

"Oh, shit, sorry, yeah." I waved a hand in Jeannie's direction. "This is my friend, Jeannie, she's joining us tonight."

"Good to know," Philip extended a hand to her, and we made our introductions. I did my best to avoid the gaze of Reno who I had last seen when I had been curled up on her bathroom floor freaking out after getting hammered off her booze. At least her opinion of me could only go up.

Jeannie soon dragged Reno off to meet a few friends of hers who were also there that evening, and left me and Philip to it once more.

"Can I get you a drink?" he asked, gesturing down at the glass in front of me, and I shook my head.

"No, I'm actually not—not that I don't, I'm just now—"

"It's cool," he said, cutting across my dithering kindly. "Mind if I get one?"

I stared at him for a moment; my stomach twisted up at the thought of him after a few drinks, no matter how good and safe and kind he seemed now. His beer breath in my face, the *come on, please, just one kiss.* I remembered Benjamin's hot, clammy breath on my hand the night before, and practically shuddered at the memory of it. I took a deep breath, as though I was about to throw myself off a cliff, which is precisely what it felt like.

"Actually, would you mind not?" I pulled a face, and he shrugged.

"Sure," he replied, without missing a beat, and I let out a sigh of relief.

"Thank you," I said and met his gaze apologetically. "I don't want to be a buzzkill, but I just—"

"Hey, I offered," he reminded me gently. "So, you ever been here before?"

The rest of the evening sped by—the polar opposite to what had gone down the night before. I even told Philip the abridged version, and he cackled along at the ridiculousness of it all and made me promise him that if he ever did anything as douchey as that I'd set off an enormous alarm in his face to keep him from making even more of a fool of himself. The band wasn't great but Philip at least seemed to know that, glancing over at me once in a while to pull faces every time they descended into another four-minute organ solo. But I didn't even care that the music was cringy or the floor was sticky or the sound system seemed to have been set up by someone keen to express their creativity through the medium of just how badly things could be fucked up. I was having a good time, and that was all because of the man standing next to me. He slipped his arm around my waist as we stood and took in the band, and I found myself drawing in against him, the warmth of his body making my pulse race. I'd forgotten just how fun this bit was, the flirting, our hands brushing together for those brief little moments and making me wonder if he'd intended that or if it was just a coincidence.

We eventually ducked away from the gig and headed back to the bar, where we spent the rest of the evening talking. Jeannie and Reno came and went, ducking in and out of our conversation with ease, as Jeannie checked in to make sure that at least this date was going a little better than the last one. It was—infinitely better. This date was on a whole other plane of reality to the one I'd been on the night before; maybe I'd worked out all my shitty date habits last night and was being rewarded by actually having a good time? Philip was smart, savagely funny, and self-effacing, and was as obsessed with pop culture and music as I was. Most of the night was spent coming back to a long, rambling debate about Ian Dury versus Ian Curtis—him on the former end, me on the latter—and in between he filled out details about his life, his work, his friends, his college years.

I couldn't remember the last time I'd had a date go so well. Usually, there was at least one point, one stutter where he would say something or do something that would get my eyes rolling or my skin crawling. I would do my best to ignore it and pretend that I hadn't noticed, but that little speck of badness would take root and usually end up blossoming into a beautiful, fruit-bearing asshole. But Philip didn't slip up, not once, not even in the eyes of dead-sober me. Our knees brushed together underneath the table and I wondered again if he was doing that on purpose.

But, while I could have sat there all night and whiled it away talking about who was more egregiously wrong about music, it was a Sunday night and both of us had to be up early to meet with clients.

"I thought freelancing meant you could do pretty much whatever you want," I said as I went to pick up my coat from the check point. He shrugged.

"I've still got clients to meet with," he explained. "It's not as easy as all that."

"It totally is, isn't it?" I teased. "You're just saying that so you can get out of this date."

"Yeah, you got me," he conceded, holding his hands up with a smile as I pulled my coat on and we headed for the door. "This has been awful. I can't wait to get away from you and be done with this already."

"So, I was on a bad date, and then I become the bad date," I said. "Poetic."

"Practically an Ian Dury lyric," he replied, and I fought the urge to dive back into that debate once more. The night was cool outside as we left the club, and Jeannie and Reno had long since headed for home. It was just the two of us on that quiet street that Sunday night. He was just a man, looking at a woman, arguing over who the best musical Ian of the twentieth century was.

He stepped towards me and slid his hand around my waist again, pulling me close, and I felt my pulse begin to pick up. I wasn't sure if that was good or bad, but I forced myself to let out a breath and relax into this. He had been so good all night, and he was so cute in those glasses, and when his gaze flicked down to my mouth I felt my stomach wriggle in the most delicious way. I wanted him. I wanted this. I closed my eyes and leaned towards him and suddenly, his mouth was on mine.

It would have been the perfect first kiss. His aftershave was musky and sweet and filled my senses as he slid his other hand around me, locking his fingers at the small of my back and drawing me against him. The cold of the air blurred with the warmth of his skin in my head, the best kind of contradiction, and his mouth was soft and gentle but firm. For a moment, I was completely lost in it, completely given over to the moment, to how right it felt and how obvious it was that the two of us had ended the night like this. His body fit around mine and I fit into his, and for a second nothing else mattered but that. But then, it came upon me like the proverbial bucket of cold water, except this cold water was a literal chunk of ice and I had just been clubbed over the head with it.

The panic bloomed fast in my chest, choking me, and I pulled away and twisted my head to the side to pull in a deep gulp of air. His hands were still linked behind my back and I reached down, cold fingers scrabbling to push him away from me.

"Is everything alright?" Philip asked, letting go of me and stepping back like he was getting out of a blast radius. I nodded, then shook my head, and then nodded again, unconvincingly.

"I'm okay, I just need to get a little air," I replied stupidly. He looked around, then turned back to me and raised his eyebrows.

"We're outside," he pointed out, and I managed a tight smile. The panic was receding, but I figured even if I went in again, I might fuck it up for a second time and that would only make things worse. I liked him, I really did, and there was nothing more in the damn world I wanted than for this to be easy—but that wasn't how it worked and I just had to accept that. I took a deep breath and forced myself to meet his gaze; he at least deserved a proper goodbye.

"I had a really good time tonight," I spoke at last, the words tumbling out of me in a great big mess that I couldn't keep a handle on. "But, I need to get home."

I darted forward, planted a kiss against his cheek, and then turned away. My heart was still racing, partly from the excitement of being close to him and partly because I wanted nothing more than to get the fuck out of there.

I stumbled around the corner, away from the bar, feeling a little drunk and not daring to look behind me in case he was following, demanding an explanation. But I didn't hear footsteps, not until I was out and halfway down the next street. When I turned to see who they belonged to I saw a handful of revellers meandering down the street from the bar I'd just come from. They put space between me and Philip, and I felt a twist of both relief and sadness in my stomach knowing that he wasn't coming after me. I didn't have to explain myself to him, but I didn't get to spend any more time around him now that I'd fucked it up this badly. I mean, we had a great date, I went in for the kiss, and then ran away like he had just tried to take a chunk out of my lower lip. He was probably just fucking bewildered, trying to make sense of where the hell he'd gone wrong. Well, at least I could be sure about where I'd fucked up.

I started the walk home, reaching into my pocket to tuck my keys between my fingers on instinct. I knew I'd have to pass through a couple of dark streets to get back to my place, and that I should have called a cab or gone back and asked Philip to walk me home. He probably would have gone with me, because he was a gentleman—no, more than that, he was a decent person. Because "gentleman" was too often used for the kind of guy who'd hold a door for you and then get mad when you didn't fucking curtsy in thanks. Philip was just a damn good human being, and that's why I wanted to walk home alone—in penance for what I'd just done, for the bullet I'd just unloaded into my own foot. I closed my eyes for a moment, a flush of humiliation and disappointment flooding my system, and forced myself to sit with it for a second before I pushed it away. Chalk it up to bad luck, and no more dates until I got myself together.

Chapter Nine

"What's that?"

Dominic nodded to my phone, which was buzzing on the table to let me know that I'd just received a new message. I raised my gaze to meet his; I was already tired of his company and it was only the beginning of the day.

"It's a phone, Dominic," I replied, deadpan, knowing that acting like an asshole to him wasn't going to help, but being unable to fight the urge to put another furrow in his brow. He rolled his eyes at me, not dignifying what I'd said with a response. It was probably for the best. I reached for my phone and checked to see who was texting me, although I already had a good idea who it was.

"What's it about?" he asked, drumming his fingers on the table in front of him. The sound bled into my brain and stuck there, and I fought the urge to slap my hand down on top of his to get him to shut the hell up.

"Nothing," I replied, tucking my phone back into my pocket when I saw that he was craning his neck to get a glance at the screen.

"Your boyfriend?" he asked, barbing the words so that they stung when they landed. I shook my head.

"No, just spam," I lied, and turned back to him. "So, did you get a chance to see them over the weekend?"

I was lying to him about the message, of course—it was something. In fact, it was a big something, the second something I'd received that morning. But I didn't want to deal with it right now.

It was in fact another message from Philip. It was Tuesday morning, and I knew that he had given me that grace period on Monday to figure things out but now, quite rightly, he wanted to know what the heck was going on. He had been sweet about it, even offering me an apology for what he had done wrong (which was nothing), but I still couldn't face getting back in contact with him yet. That would mean having to accept the ridiculous fuckery I'd pulled on what should have been the best first date I'd ever been on.

So, I found myself stuck in that room with nowhere to go even inside my own head, watching Dominic as he marched back and forth in front of me, holding court on exactly how I was wrong about The Tantrums. I steepled my fingers and focused on the sensation of my fingertips pressing together, doing my best not to let him get to me. It wasn't working.

"No, I didn't," he said, shaking his head. "I was off seeing this other band, and I really think you should give them a listen."

"Okay, what are they like?" I tried to sound perky and enthusiastic but instead it came out hollow and lilting, like I was trying to play a guitar that hadn't been tuned in weeks.

"It's these four guys from San Francisco," he began enthusiastically, spreading his hands wide like he was delivering me them on a platter. "The album they're working on now is sort of a concept one about a break-up…"

Static filled my head as soon as he got to that part. As though we didn't have enough bands on our roster made up of four guys writing concept albums about their break-ups that were really just thinly-veiled excuses to crap all over the women who'd dared dump men as exceptional as them.

"I don't know, maybe I just relate to them," Dominic finished up, and I felt this doomed sensation overtake me as I realized he was about to *share stuff* with me. "I just went through a break-up myself…"

He left the end of the sentence hanging in the air between us, like he was expecting me to cock my head to the side and sweetly press for more. Well, I had bad news for him. After that catastrophic date with Benjamin, I had lost my tolerance for pretending to be politely interested in men's bullshit. I stayed silent, and he shot a glance in my direction, as though he wasn't sure that I'd heard what he said.

"So, what kind of music do they do?" I asked, a little twisted part of me enjoying the fact that I had refused to rise to his attempts to wring sympathy out of me. I would ask about his life the next time he bothered to ask about mine, and I still wasn't certain that he even knew my last name, so that might be a while yet.

"Just classic guitar-driven indie rock stuff," he replied, and I could see by the way that he slid his gaze away from mine that he knew what my answer was going to be.

"You know that's not really selling right now," I pointed out. "And besides, it's not as though we're short on bands like that on our roster at the moment."

"I guess," he muttered, seeming irritated that I'd had the temerity to point it out.

"But The Tantrums, on the other hand," I said, bringing the conversation back around to the point I'd been making. "They're new, they're interesting, they're writing about stuff that I'm not seeing anywhere else at the moment. I really think you should give them a listen."

"They just don't excite me." He waved his hand, like that was that, and I felt this hot burst of irritation flash into my head.

"Pretty much none of the bands you've brought in here the last six months have excited me, but I've given them all a fair shot," I pointed out. I wanted to get to my feet and slam my hands down on the table and raise my voice, just like he had done earlier in the day when we'd been arguing about a different group, but I knew that as soon as I did that he would feel free to write me off as overly attached. And maybe I was, because this group had become a sticking point for me. Every time he brushed them off, those three girls and their weird little songs about movies and growing up in the Midwest, my resolve towards them only hardened. I wondered how many other record labels they'd gone through, losing out on contracts because some guy just got dumped and wanted to wallow in his sadness with another white-boy concept album on regret. Well, not this time.

"Fine." Dominic let out this long sigh, and I quelled the urge to remind him that this was his job. "I'll give them a listen."

"You know what, I'll get them out now," I said. I fired up my laptop and went to find the folder of music that contained their stuff. "Since it seems to keep slipping your mind when you're out of the office."

"I'm going for a cigarette break," he replied bluntly, a pout almost forming on his face as he got to his feet. "And then I'm taking lunch. Maybe when I get back?"

"Yeah, maybe," I muttered, watching as he headed for the door and left me with my cursor hovering over the "play" button. Typical. As soon as he might have to give a second's thought to something I liked, he found an excuse to duck out of here. Maybe I could just set up the EP to go through the building's speakers so he couldn't avoid it. But even then, he'd probably rather plug up his ears and listen to himself go on about his own problems instead.

Maybe I should have been a little more sympathetic, but I couldn't find it in me for the time being. I looked down at my phone to check the time, and saw the message from Philip sitting there and waiting for me; I felt a twist of guilt in my stomach as I read the words again. I should get back to him. But I just wasn't sure how.

I had hoped—some stupid part of me had hoped, at least—that once I accepted that I needed therapy I would step out from under the darkness of what had happened to me and get on with it. But that kiss had reminded me that I wasn't ready for any of the physical stuff that came with dating yet. And, unless I conducted most of my romantic relationships from inside a big plastic ball, boy-in-the-bubble style, that was going to be a problem. Philip didn't deserve to be dragged through my dumbass neuroses. He was too sweet a guy for that nonsense.

It felt like a cruel joke on top of a crueler one, that the universe should dump this perfect guy at my feet mere weeks after something too big for me to handle had happened. If I'd met him a month or two before, maybe it would have been different—fuck, maybe I never would have been out with Kieran that night and it wouldn't have happened in the first place. I pushed that thought from my head. Those kind of hot takes were getting me nowhere.

The words on the screen thrummed hard against my head, and part of me wanted nothing more than to call him up, tell him I had lost my charger, and ask him to meet up for lunch that afternoon. But I couldn't do that. Not yet. Not now.

And not least because I was meant to be meeting Irina for something to eat in twenty minutes. I closed my laptop, tucked it into my bag, and headed out of the office. I did my best not to wonder if Philip was out there somewhere, frowning at his phone and wondering why I hadn't bothered to reply.

Chapter Ten

"I swear to God, Dominic, just one song! That's all I'm asking!"

I threw my hands in the air, and realized that Dominic was looking at me with an expression I'd never seen before—one that I was about to get a blunt lesson in the context of. But the first thing I thought of when I saw the way he was looking at me was the conversation I'd had with Jeannie over the weekend, about his refusal to actually listen to The Tantrums or indeed any of the bands that I actually rated.

I felt as though I had been having the same conversation with him for weeks, the very definition of insanity, as nothing seemed to change no matter how I approached it. At least this shit with Dominic had been enough to get my mind off of what was going on, or not going on, with Philip. It had been over a week since our last date, and seething over Dominic was the distraction I needed—even if it left me fuming enough to go rant to Jeannie about work.

"You know he's just doing this to get one over on you, right?" she had pointed out, just before I plugged in my headphones to listen to another band that he wanted me to check out. "He's not going to give your band a minute just because you're doing that for him."

"I know, but I need to be professional," I sighed. "I don't want to lose my job."

"Oh, fuck your job," she said, waving her hand cheerfully. "Start your own place, and make your first port of call rejecting every dude who has a misogynistic break-up album about how his ex is a whore."

"Would that I could." I sighed deeply, pushing the jack into the hole and lifting the earbuds up. Because even though I guess I knew somewhere deep in my stomach that she was right, I still believed that Dominic genuinely respected my opinions and wouldn't just dismiss them out of hand. Well, I had believed it, right until I walked back into work on Monday morning and found that he still hadn't even bothered to listen to the EP I'd sent him. Now we were back rehashing the same argument yet again, after returning from lunch.

"They're just not right for us," he protested, holding his hands up. I planted my hands on my hips; I was on my feet, and I wasn't going to let him talk down to me a moment longer. Jeannie was right. He never had any intention of paying mind to the bands that I liked. Now that I thought of it, really cast my mind back over every single group we had signed over the years, it seemed that more and more of them were just the groups that he liked, the ones that I happened to agree on. Everything that I'd floated myself had been either shot down or dismissed out of hand. He never tried. He never respected me. I was just there to bolster his opinion when he needed it.

"What, you don't think an innovative, different, popular group is right for us?" I demanded. "They've got a big following, even if you don't like them. We'd easily make our money back if we produced—"

"It's not just about the money though, is it?" he cut me off, his voice so painfully patronising it was all I could do not to lean across and rip his tongue out of his fucking head. "It's about the musicality of it."

"And how would you know anything about that if you've never fucking listened to them?" I demanded, my voice rising again. I didn't give a shit. Maybe if I yelled it at him, he'd actually get it through his dumb head that I wasn't here as fucking decoration. I realized that my chest was rising and falling quickly, and did my best to center myself. I didn't want him to be able to dismiss me as nothing more than a hysterical woman hell-bent on proving a point, even if that was an accurate description of my mood right then.

"Hey, you need to calm down," he said. He stepped towards me and, to my shock, grabbed my arms as though trying to keep me in check—like I was taking up too much space and by pinning my arms to my sides he could keep me from busting out of the little corner of this business that he'd assigned me. I shook my head, and tried to step back from him.

"Let go of me," I snapped, but he held tighter, standing in front of me, his hands digging into my elbows. I felt the panic rise again, familiar to me now, but this time it was meshed with anger and the mixture of the two was—

What.

That was the only word in my head when he leaned in to kiss me. It was the only word I could find anywhere in my entire brain. Not a question, even, just a statement, a demand. His mouth was on mine and his grip was tightening on my arms and my head felt as though it had been bleached blank. I was back in that apartment, his hands pushing up my skirt; I was in the gig, the other guy's hands snaking over my ass. I was a dozen places at once, all their hands on me, their gazes, their comments, sick to my stomach with humiliation and anger and what I should have said, what I could have done. It wasn't enough. It never was. My body wasn't mine as soon as they touched me; I became public property. I was stuck between crawling out of my skin and being trapped hopelessly within it as he tried to pry my mouth open with his tongue, his breath hot on my skin. The moment seemed to last forever, my body marble under his fingers, unfeeling, unthinking, his to shape.

I felt his hand working its way clumsily to the front of my body, fumbling with the fly of my jeans, and the shock dropped away and I managed to yank myself from his grasp.

"No," I said, stepping away, but his hand was still clutching my arm. The word felt small in the face of what I was feeling, but it was enough—a start. He looked up at me, and as soon as he realized that I wasn't fucking around, he dropped my elbow at once. His face fell with it.

"I'm sorry, I'm sorry, I'm sorry," he burbled as I dived away from him, pressing myself against the back wall, putting as much space as I could put between the two of us without walking straight out of the room. "I'm sorry, I thought you wanted—"

"Stop!" I held my hand up. I could only manage one word at a time, but it was all I needed for now. I took a deep breath; my head was screaming with feeling and I couldn't shut it up. Dominic stood there, his face contorted with worry and something that looked like regret. Despite myself, I felt a twist of sympathy for him; I knew that he deserved this, that he had been the one to grab me without asking, but I still, stupidly, wanted to tell him that it was alright.

"What the fuck did you think you were doing?" I demanded, and he shrugged and shook his head, like a kid caught with his hand in the cookie jar.

"I don't know," he admitted. "I just…you were so… passionate…"

"You thought because I was showing emotion of any kind that meant that I must want your fucking dick?" I snapped, my voice pitching up with incredulity. "You really thought…?"

Words escaped me, and he took a step towards me once more.

"There's always been something between us, Edie," he murmured, his voice urgent, and he caught my chin in his fingers and tilted my face up so I had to look at him. I jerked my head back, this time the fury unambiguous. All those impotent brush-offs I had forced myself to give before roiled up inside me, the foaming crest of the wave finally coming down on the man before me.

"Get off of me," I snarled, twisting away from him. "Don't you dare come fucking *anywhere* near me again, you understand?"

"Edie, please—" He tried to speak again, but I didn't want to hear it. If I never heard his voice again it would be too soon, and if I did it would probably be telling me that a band that I liked were derivative and uninspired.

"Go screw yourself, fuckhead," I muttered, grabbing my stuff and shoving it quickly into my bag. I brushed by him, barging out and into the corridor, and then down the hallway and out of the building until there were a few hundred feet between me and the man who had just put his unwelcome hands on me.

I gulped great lungfuls of air as soon as I was outside, and realized that there were tears pricking my eyes. I blinked them away; I might have just had to fight off yet another man who wouldn't take no for an answer but the thought of letting anyone see that it had upset me was somehow worse. Having to explain, in so many words, what had happened, would have made it real, and I couldn't bear the thought of accepting that another man in my life had put his hands on me in *that* way. Were there any men left who knew what the fuck the word "no" meant?

And then, my thoughts flashed to the phone in my pocket. To the messages from Philip, which I had left unanswered, unsure of what to say to explain how I had reacted to what had happened on our last date. There was at least one decent guy left, but I had left him on hold since our first real outing together.

Fuck it. I reached into my pocket and pulled out my phone; there was no harm in giving him a try. I needed to restore my faith in men before it dissolved completely and I just ended up retiring to my apartment with Max and a pair of headphones for company. I clicked on his messages and quickly tapped out a reply. I knew I wasn't going back to work, so I suggested we meet. A quick apology, a question of time and place, and I sent it before I had a chance to wonder if what I was doing was a bad idea or not.

I dropped the phone back into my bag and headed down the street, not looking back at the office and not caring one bit if they were mad at me for leaving. Dominic could explain why I had stormed out—in great detail, preferably. I didn't have to put up with his shit, and if they took his side over mine, then maybe I should just walk out for good.

I was heading in the vague direction of my apartment, but I was so high on the adrenalin from what Dominic had tried to do to me that I couldn't focus on direction so well. It wasn't until my phone buzzed against my waist that I realized that I had come to a halt on a street corner, staring into space, my eyes drying in the afternoon air. I blinked, reached into my bag, and looked at my phone. It was Philip.

"Sure," he had agreed at once. "Where are you? I'm in the city right now with nothing to do."

I looked up at the street sign above me, my heart looping at the spontaneity of it; nothing seemed to make more sense in that moment that letting him come out to meet me, even if I didn't deserve his attention or energy after all the shit I'd pulled over the last week. The thought of him close to me was enough to blot out the weight that had descended on my shoulders.

"Coffee shop? Same one we met in?" I fired back, and bit my lip to keep the big, goofy grin busting out all over my face.

"See you there in ten," he replied, and I dropped my phone back into my bag and hurried to make it there in time. I'd already kept him waiting long enough—the least I could do was be early for what was to be our second proper date.

Chapter Eleven

WHEN I GOT THERE, THE PLACE WAS QUIET, quiet enough that I could claim the comfy seats next to the window. I cursed myself for leaving my book at home this morning; I would have liked to be casually flicking through something unthreateningly intellectual when he got here, looking like I was lost in my reading, but instead I found myself perched on the edge of my seat peering out the window and watching for when he arrived. I felt a little dorky, but I didn't care. This was the distraction I needed, something to pour all that excess nervous energy into after what had happened with Dominic just a few minutes before. I could still feel his grip on my elbow, and I found my fingertips drifting to my arm as though to mimic the feeling of his hand on me, or to replace it. I rubbed the spot absently, eyes glazing over as I found myself back in the moment, but before I could get too far lost in that feeling again, my gaze focused on Philip. He grinned when he saw me waiting there for him, and ducked through the door and took a seat opposite me.

"Long time no see," he remarked, as I offered him an apologetic smile.

"Honestly, I had a whole bunch of excuses about my charger being broken and stuff, but I've just had a lot going on the last couple of weeks," I admitted. "I'm sorry I didn't get back to you; that was shitty of me."

"Yeah, kind of," he said, and then glanced up to the counter. "What do you want to drink?"

"I want to buy," I said, getting to my feet. "I think it's the least I can do after keeping you waiting so long."

"In that case I'll have everything they've got in the biggest size," he teased, then gave me his real order. I returned with a couple of coffees, placing his carefully in front of him; the mug wobbled dangerously on the saucer and as he reached up to steady it, his hand brushed against mine and my skin sang where we'd made the connection. I slipped back into my seat opposite him and he regarded me for a moment before speaking again.

"So, why the spontaneous date?" he asked. "I thought most real people were working this time of day."

"I was," I admitted. "I just had, ah, I had a half-day thing. Unexpectedly. And I wasn't ready to go home yet."

"Sounds like you're cutting class," he remarked, cocking an eyebrow, but I waved my hand at him.

"Nothing for you to worry about," I assured him. I really didn't want to go into what had happened with Dominic, and why it had caused such a tectonic reaction in me. This was a second date, not a support group meeting.

"What about you?" I prodded him with my foot under the low table that sat between us as he began to drink his coffee. "Don't you freelancers have to work twenty-four-seven to make ends meet?"

"Yeah, this little meeting means I won't be able to make rent this month," he said, shrugging casually. "But it was worth it."

"You barely just got here…"

"Still worth it," he replied, flashing me a smile, and the world looped around me since I was the focus of it. I smiled back, then returned my attention to my coffee.

"So, what do you want to do?" he asked, glancing out of the window behind him. "We've got the whole day and the whole city out there."

"I have no idea," I admitted. "This was kind of last-minute. And I'm not very good at last-minute."

"Well, I'm procrastinating from work for this," he replied. "So, I'm going to make this last as long as I can, if that's alright with you."

"Fine by me!" I held my hands up. The last thing I wanted right now was to go back to that empty apartment and sit there and dwell on what had happened and how I was going to deal with it. I knew I would have to eventually, but for the time being I would take whatever company I could get. Not to mention the fact that there was something nice about being around someone who had no idea about any of my issues, who didn't regard me once in a while with that sadness and sorrowfulness that put my teeth on edge.

"There's a movie theatre that opened up not far from my apartment," he remarked, jerking his head in what I assumed was the direction of his home base. "I've been looking for an excuse to check it out."

"Excuse provided," I replied, lifting my coffee cup to his; he leaned over and chinked his mug against mine, and this time I couldn't keep the smile off my face. Okay, so maybe this day could actually be salvageable yet.

The rest of the date, because I guessed that's what I had to admit that it was, flew by so fast that I hardly had time to stop and think about what had gotten me out of work in the first place. It felt weird, initially, to be out of the office on a weekday like this, but soon enough I settled into it. Philip took me to this movie theatre, a little indie place with a bar and restaurant that served overpriced hipster appetizers that we split and giggled over before our film began. The movie was cute and short, some little foreign animation film with jangly music and a dog who reminded me of the Dalmatian I'd had when I was a kid. Afterwards, we headed somewhere a little less snobby for dinner, happening upon a diner that was open twenty-four hours; the waitress looked as though she'd be on for every minute of that shift, and was surly and short with us but we didn't care. We were too busy talking: about the movie, about movies in general, about books, TV, music, hometowns, high school. The conversation had started in the coffee shop and spread out down the street and followed us from venue to venue. Most dates I went on, there were at least a handful of awkward pauses, of "So, tell me about your..." moments, but there was nothing like that with Philip. He was so easy to talk to, easy to be around, that when he reached out to take my hand as we headed out of the cinema, I let him. His skin was warm against mine, and there was something comforting about his touch; I didn't want to whip my hand away like I had done with the other guys who'd tried to get their hands on me before. He just felt...good. Right.

It was something like relief, knowing that I could actually be touched by someone like him again; the other guys, Dominic and Benjamin, had obviously just been the universe letting me know that now wasn't the right time, or they weren't the right people. Philip was right. I linked my arm through his as we walked out of the diner, and tipped my head back to look at the darkening sky; I would have to go into work tomorrow, no matter what had happened today, and I didn't like the thought of facing up to whatever I had to face up to on only a few hours' sleep.

"I should probably be getting back to my place," I remarked, a little reluctant. I didn't want this day to end, but I knew that unless I invited him to stay the night that

I would have to say goodbye. And I just wasn't sure I was ready for that yet; I didn't want to push my boundaries, especially after what had happened earlier in the day. Although, when I looked at him now, under the sharp citrus glow of the streetlights above us, I felt this twist of longing in my stomach. Desire. I wanted him, even if I knew it wasn't a good idea. *But when had that made hooking up any less tempting?*

"I'll walk you back if you want," he offered, ever the gentleman. I paused for a moment, wondering if it was a good idea, but figured that it would be better to have him here with me than not. I just wanted to squeeze in a few more moments of his company wherever I could find them.

"Yeah, I do," I said. I smiled at him, and pointed my chin in the direction of my apartment. "This way."

We walked and talked, and I deliberately took a longer route than I normally would have, not ready to bid farewell to him quite yet. But eventually we arrived outside my door, and I didn't have any excuses in my arsenal for us to circle to block once more.

"This you?" He looked up at the building.

"Yeah, this is me," I nodded, reaching into my bag to pull out my keys. I kept my hand tucked into his arm, not ready to break free yet.

"I had a really awesome day today," he said, smiling at me and watching as I pulled my keys from my bag. "We should do this again sometime."

"Yeah, I won't be fake-losing my charger again any time soon," I promised him. Finally, I pulled my hand free of his arm, and the two of us stood there for a moment, just looking at each other. We had nothing left to say. My pulse picked up slightly, the blood in my veins heating a little. Any other date, and I would have been going in for a kiss.

Fuck, any other date and I would already have him up in my apartment.

Fuck it. Before I could stop myself, I moved towards him and pressed my lips against his. He slipped his hands around my waist at once, like he had done the last time, linking his fingers behind the small of my back, but this time the gesture didn't make me feel trapped. It made me feel safe, secure, contained; I wrapped my arms around his neck and kissed him hard, our tongues meeting and our bodies connecting and my skin prickling with the sheer level of my want for him. I could have stood there all night and made out with him, just to prove to myself that I could, that I was in control of my body and its reactions. But I wanted more. I wanted to see how far I could take this.

"Come upstairs?" I asked breathlessly, pulling back and fluttering my eyes open to look at him. There was something a little darker in his gaze now, deeper.

"Hell, yes," he agreed, and leaned in to kiss me again, as though he couldn't get enough; I knew we were out on a busy street and that someone could walk by and catch us at any minute, but I didn't care. If anything, that just made it hotter. He slid a hand up my back and let it rest at the sensitive spot at the nape of my neck, and I shivered at his touch. Before I could let this go any further while the two of us were still in prime indecent exposure territory, I remembered the keys in my hand and went to unlock the door. I glanced over my shoulder at him, the very definition of a come-hither look, and he didn't need telling twice, following me up the stairs and into my apartment.

Once we were inside, it didn't take long for things to kick up a notch in intensity; I thanked God that Max had fallen asleep on the couch and wasn't going to make a scene about there being another man in the apartment. I led Philip straight into the bedroom, our mouths meeting sporadically as we both undressed as quickly as we could. Part of me was in a panic that the bad feelings would catch up with me if I stopped for so much as a second, and that meant I had to keep going, full-throttle, no pauses for air. I swivelled around and tugged my hair out of the way so he could undo my bra, and the feeling of his fingertips brushing against the skin of my back was enough to draw a moan from between my lips. Fuck. How had I managed to go without this for so long?

He pulled off my bra, himself stripped down to his underwear, and pushed me back on to the bed. His breath was coming quickly and I could feel him, hard, beneath the fabric that separated us. I lifted my hips to press myself against him, hooking my ankles behind his back to pull him in closer as he made his way down my neck, towards my breasts, flicking his tongue out against each one of my nipples in turn. I loved that he wanted to take his time, but I needed this. I needed to prove to myself that I could do this.

"Fuck me," I panted in his ear, hoping that he wasn't one of those guys who insisted on inching over every minute detail of your body before they actually bothered to get down to business. But Philip simply raised his head, kissed me again, and slid his hand down my body to part my legs.

"Whatever you say," he grinned, and I reached into the small cabinet by my bed to pull out a condom and pressed it into his hand. Shifting up the bed, I felt a little squirm of nervousness and excitement in my stomach as I watched him pull off his underwear and sheath himself; his cock was thick and stout, and I could already imagine what it would feel like inside me. Wriggling out of my own underwear, I lay back on the bed and shot him my best fuck-me look.

"Fuck, you look good like that," he murmured, and slid on top of me, pushing one thigh back a little so he could position himself at the entrance to my slit. My heartrate picked up again. I felt him nudge up against me, the head of his cock spreading me—and then, a jolt of pain.

"Ah," I winced, and he stopped.

"Is everything alright?" he asked, a furrow appearing between his eyebrows. I nodded.

"Yeah, yeah, it's fine," I shifted my hips down a little, hoping that a change in angle might make things better. "Go again, go again."

He pushed into me once more, and this time the pain was more immediate—a raw, scraping feeling, like someone was trying to pry me apart.

"Fuck," I squirmed beneath him, the pain giving rise to panic in my chest.

"Are you okay?" He leaned back, observing me with concern. I nodded, arching my back to try and take him again. But as soon as he was inside me, the pain came back, lancing through me, impossible to ignore or push through. I gritted my teeth and tried to let him go deeper, but it felt as though someone was trying to fit their entire leg inside me. It hurt like *hell*. My natural instinct was to bat him away, stop the source of the pain anyway I knew how, but if I ever wanted to have sex again I would just have to push through it-

"Fuck, ow," I pulled away from him, closing my legs and rocking to the side. I couldn't take it. It just hurt too badly. He looked down at me, confusion clouding his features.

"What's wrong?" he asked. "If you don't want to do this…"

"No, I want to do this," I assured him, leaning up to kiss him again.

"Then why are you…"

"I don't know," I snapped in response, and then closed my eyes. Frustration, anger, the remnants of the pain, they were all flickering through my head like frames from a bad movie. None of them were exactly conducive to a session of hot, boundaryless screwing.

"We don't have to do anything you don't want to," he assured me, and I felt that flare of irritation again, not at him, but at myself—because I *did* want to do this. I did. I knew I did. My brain wanted him, but my body had slammed its doors shut in the face of both of us and I had no idea why. I felt like someone was trying to prop me open with a brick.

I curled my legs up underneath me, tugging the covers over myself, and noticed that Max was standing in the doorway to the bedroom, frozen still, staring at both of us with a scandalized expression on his little furry face. I snorted with laughter, momentarily distracted from the embarrassment of what had just happened. Philip glanced over his shoulder and grinned when he saw Max standing there and peering at us like a disapproving parent, and then looked back over to me. I tugged the covers up and over myself, covering my body up.

"I'm assuming this isn't going to happen, then?" He gestured down to the condom, and I nodded sadly.

"It's nothing to do with you," I promised him, even though I wasn't certain I was telling the truth. Nothing like this had ever happened to me before, and I had no fucking clue where it had come from.

"What is it to do with?" he asked, his tone patient but tinged with frustration; I knew how he felt. I was there myself.

"I don't know," I said, shaking my head. "I...this hasn't happened before. It just...hurt, when you tried to..."

I gestured down at him as he pulled the rest of the covers around his body. He looked good naked; I was almost glad we'd had to stop things, because it gave me a chance to admire his body, toned but not absurd, in the dim light coming from the streetlamp outside my window.

"Yeah, I got that," he sighed, reaching over and taking my hand. The physical connection was a comfort, a promise that he wasn't going to walk out of here because I couldn't give him what I wanted.

"It's never happened before," I explained again quickly, sounding distinctly like the time that my college boyfriend had lost his boner before he could screw me and had spent the rest of the night following me around my apartment all but begging me to tell him that it was normal and that it would never happen again.

"Then why has it started now?" he asked, and the frustration was beginning to fade from his voice. I hated the fact that I loved how understanding he was being, that he wasn't pushing for this to go ahead despite what had happened. I knew so many guys—hell, had slept with so many guys—for whom my pain would have been nothing more than a roadblock in the way to getting their dick wet: a roadblock they would have driven straight through.

"I don't..." I was going to repeat myself again, was going to tell him once more that I didn't know why this had happened, but I knew damn straight that it would be a lie. I knew why this had happened. I just didn't want to have to face up to it. I closed my eyes, stopped myself mid-sentence, and took a big, long breath, like I was setting myself up once more to jump off a cliff edge.

"I think there's something I need to tell you," I mumbled, averting my eyes from his. And then, without giving myself any more time to overthink it, I told him. I told him everything.

Chapter Twelve

I WOKE THE NEXT MORNING, blinking into the light streaming in through the skylight above my bed, and stretched my arms around wide—only to find them bumping up against the man in bed next to me. I turned and looked at Philip, blinking the sleep from my eyes, and smiled. He was here. He was really, actually, truly still here.

I hadn't expected him to stay after everything I'd told him. I had expected him to up and get out of there as soon as he had the chance, and I wouldn't have blamed him one little bit if he had. It was our second date, for the love of God, and I had just dumped a huge pile of shittiness on his head and expected him to just up and deal with it.

And, somehow, he had. The whole time I was telling him—about the incident, about getting drunk and freaking out at a stranger's house, about the therapy—I felt as though someone else had taken control of my tongue. Some part of me was watching, horrified, and hissing at me to shut the hell up before I scared this near-perfect guy away for good. I wished I could say there was another part of me, one overriding that, that knew this was the right thing to do and trusted him not to run out on me, but there wasn't. I just had to plug through it, to ignore the dumbass voices in my head that were telling me that I was going to scare him away. *No man in their right mind would want to handle the shit you're bringing to the table. Tuck it down, deep down, and let him fuck you.*

But he stayed. He didn't say much—I could tell he was angry, not at me but at the story I was telling, but he seemed to understand that the last thing I needed right now was him going all white knight on my ass and heading out into the night to go after the guy who had done it to me in the first place. But when I was all done telling him, he pulled me into his arms and balanced his chin on top of my head. The weight of his body against mine was a comfort, and the steady thud of his heartbeat below my ear was all I needed right then. Just someone to tell me without words that it was going to be alright and that they weren't going anywhere.

I wanted so badly to be the perfect woman for him. I did for every man I'd been with, twisting myself up and around to fit their taste in music and love the movies they loved and get along with all their shittiest friends to show that I was game. And, for as long as the day had lasted, I had just about managed to convince myself that I could be that for Philip. It had felt good, the knowledge that I pleased him and that I could crush down everything that had been screwing things up for me the last few months and make like it wasn't there at all. But now something unavoidable had manifested itself, and I couldn't convince myself or him that this was going to be smooth sailing.

"Just so you know," he finally spoke, when he had me all wrapped up in his arms and Max was sitting on the end of the bed cheerily cleaning the pads of his paws like none of this was happening. "That's not a problem."

"Are you sure?" I peeled myself away from him and looked him in the eye. "Because I don't know…I don't know how long any of this is going to go on."

"I'm sure," he replied firmly, pulling me back against his chest and planting a brief kiss on my temple.

"You can go whenever you want," I promised him. "I won't hold it against you."

"You totally would," he replied cheerfully, the frustration that had tinged his tone earlier gone completely. We lay there for a moment, and Philip reached out to scratch Max behind the ear; Max enthusiastically pressed his head into Philip's hand, letting out a happy little chirrup now that he was finally getting the attention he clearly felt like he deserved.

"You know, my parents always told me never to trust anyone who didn't love animals," he remarked, as Max flipped over on to his side and began batting playfully at Philip's fingers. "Because, you know, animals are innocents and people who don't like them must be bitter assholes. I guess the fact that you've got a cat means I can trust you."

"Was that the tipping point?" I asked, and he nodded.

"Yeah, up until I saw him I wasn't sure if you were going to murder me and make a hat out of my skin or something, but I'm pretty confident now."

"A hat out of your skin?"

"Haven't you ever seen Hannibal?"

And just like that the two of us were lost in conversation once more, conversation that stretched out over the rest of the night until I could barely keep my eyes open and found myself slipping into sleep once more. And when I woke up next to him, I realized it was the best rest I'd had in months—since The Thing had happened.

Any other day, I might have rolled over and woken him up with a kiss on the back of the neck and indulged in some lazy morning sex before I had to leave for work, but I didn't know if my vagina was still being a dick. *My vagina's acting like a dick.* That was a new one on me.

I checked the time—it was early, the light streaming through the window with that crisp, cold sunshine of a late-fall morning. I rolled out of bed and headed for the shower, and practically swooned at the cuteness when I saw that

Max was curled up against Philip's leg. Philip might have only trusted people who liked animals, but I only trusted people who my animal liked. I scratched the spot between Max's ears and snuck off to the bathroom to shower and get myself ready for work. I still had to go back in today, no matter how desperately I didn't want to. The thought of facing Dominic today was just galling, especially after the events of last night. I knew it wasn't true, but I couldn't help but feel like it was his touch that had gotten my vagina to slam shut in the face of having sex again. As soon as I'd felt his fingers scrabbling at my crotch, it was like someone had nailed up boards down there and declared the whole place abandoned, just to keep him out.

I showered quickly and wandered into the kitchen, wondering if there was anything in there I could use so that Philip would find me sexily making breakfast when he got up, but he had beaten me to the punch.

"Morning," he greeted me, and I turned to find him standing in his underwear and leaning against the arch that led through to the kitchen. Max was at his feet, either trying to get his attention for more cuddles or to murder him by getting in the way of his footfalls.

"Morning," I said in return. I felt my heart flutter at the sight of him, forgetting for a moment everything that had gone wrong the night before and focusing only on what had gone right. I reached out my arms and he stepped towards me obligingly, wrapping his arms around me and holding me close. I closed my eyes and let myself enjoy the feeling for a moment, this single, uncomplicated moment.

"I should be getting off to work soon," I mumbled reluctantly against his chest, but he didn't move.

"Well, I don't have anywhere to be, and I fully intend on hanging out with your cat all day," he replied.

"I'm sure he'd love that, but your procrastination has gone on long enough," I teased. "You want to go out for a coffee?"

"That sounds perfect," he agreed, and we both got dressed and headed out of the apartment, hand in hand. It felt a little stupid to be as excited as I was to be walking about with him like this, like a real couple, but I didn't care. It had been a long, shitty few months, and I would take the little flashes of unfettered happiness where I could find them.

We drank our coffees and talked about everything except what had happened the night before; I didn't blame him, since the last thing I wanted was to have to think about what had gone down (or hadn't). I hadn't even told him about the thing with Dominic, either, mainly because it felt as though I had dumped enough exhausting bullshit on his doorstep for the time being—but partly because I was a little worried that he actually might not believe me. Something about curating all those incidences into one big story made it feel to me like I was making it all up. Like I was showing off, in some sick way: *look at all these men who want me so much they didn't even stop to ask.* I suspected he would never have seen it that way, and if I had so much as hinted in that direction around Jeannie or one of my other friends they would tear me a new one, but still. It was different when it came to me, for some reason.

"I had a really good time last night," I said, lingering outside the coffee shop, not caring much about the cold that was numbing my fingers. "Sorry, that sounds so cheesy..."

"No, I did too," he replied. "And...I meant what I said. I really like you, Edie, and I don't want to go anywhere."

"You have no idea how happy that makes me," I said, sighing. He planted a soft kiss on my lips, the kind that I knew I would be feeling for the rest of the day every time I thought of him.

"See you later?"

"See you later," I nodded. "And this time I'll actually reply to your texts."

"Good to know," he grinned, and turned to leave me to cover the rest of the distance between the coffee shop and work.

The pain of the night before—literal and otherwise—was still lingering at the back of my head, but I shoved it down to be dealt with later, maybe in another therapy session once I had figured out all of this shit with work. I needed to keep my head forward and my mind in the game for the next few hours, because I had a feeling that it was going to be rough.

I arrived at the office earlier than I usually did, and was disappointed to see Dominic's motorbike waiting outside; he was already in. I had wanted some extra time in our shared office to myself, but that wasn't going to happen. I felt a creeping sense of dread crawling up the back of my neck; something was different. Something was wrong. And I didn't like where this was headed.

I came in, inhaling that familiar scent of citrus and pine and nodding to Lindsay, the receptionist, hoping that clinging to the familiar details would keep me from getting too hung up in my own anxiety. I still remembered when I'd first walked in here, fresh off an internship and straight out of my final term studying marketing at college, all New Wave obsessions and certainty that I was going to be the one to change this industry from the inside out. I mean, I hadn't quite achieved that—in fact, most of the time, I found myself dealing with bands that were all but interchangeable, jangly guitar rock from Midwestern guys with clean-cut, marketable looks and cocky attitudes. But I still remembered walking in here and feeling like this was my chance to make a real difference, to change the music world. It was a shame I still hadn't delivered on that yet.

I headed through to the office that Dominic and I shared—I had to go past maybe a half-dozen offices of duos the same as the two of us. The label was obsessed with two people working together, especially a man and a woman, as though sticking two opinionated people with equal say to work together on something as nebulous as music was a good idea. I wondered how many of them had ended up in fights like this, how many had hooked up or broken up or had to deal with aggressive come-ons from their other halves.

I paused outside the door to our office. It had his name on it, but not mine; I always hated that, even though the higher-ups assured me that it didn't mean anything and wasn't an indication of job security or anything like that. But it was a reminder that I could be ousted at any moment and they wouldn't have to change a thing to undo my existence in this place at all. I put my hand on the door and walked in, tilting my chin up and hoping to God that I conveyed something close to confidence.

"Edie, hi!" A voice I didn't recognize greeted me; I blinked a couple of times and found myself faced with Kathleen Tennison, one of the HR people. I'd seen her once on my first day here, and had hoped then that I wouldn't do anything that would bring us back into contact again. Dominic was standing a little behind her, as though he wanted to use her as a human shield against my detonation. The dread returned. This wasn't good.

"Hi, Kathleen," I greeted her, shooting a look at Dominic that let him know that I knew damn well what his game was here. He had once again beaten me into the office, gotten the drop on me, and pulled in someone higher up than either of us to make it so we couldn't just figure out what had happened yesterday between the two of us.

"Do you want to take a seat?" She gestured to the other side of the desk in front of her, but I stayed standing. Sitting down, with the two of them towering over me, would have felt like I was admitting some wrongdoing, like I was an errant schoolgirl getting scolded. I shook my head.

"I'm good," I replied. "Is this about what happened yesterday?"

"Yes," Kathleen nodded, and I glared at Dominic again. Spineless little fucking toad. He could have dealt with this to my face but probably didn't trust himself not to misread the signals again.

"What do we need to talk about?" I asked, feeling a flare of rage that lifted me out of my body for a moment.

"You left the office yesterday," she continued gently, her tone the auditory equivalent of kid gloves. "We need to talk about why that was."

"Have you asked him?" I demanded, nodding towards Dominic. He inched his eyes away from me, looking at the doorknob behind me. I crossed my arms across my chest in a fury.

"Dominic came to us with concern after what happened yesterday," she went on, every word out of her mouth sounding carefully curated.

"That he tried to stick his hand down my pants?" I snapped back. Her face flickered with the barest hint of surprise, but she swiftly wiped it away.

"We know that the two of you shared a…shared a moment," she nodded, shooting a look in Dominic's direction that told him he was in trouble for not mentioning that to her. "And obviously, the fact that you left work afterwards without clearing it with anyone is something we need to talk about. As you know, relationships between employees..."

"We haven't got a relationship!" I shook my head, exasperated. "We just work together. That's it. Seriously."

"Things clearly took a turn for the physical yesterday, regardless," she replied patiently. She was talking like she thought I was trying to keep something quiet—like I was trying to protect him, or myself, or worse, the two of us as an entity.

"And Dominic was honest enough to come to me and discuss that." She glanced over at him, and he nodded quickly, as though acknowledging her thanks. I wanted to punch him.

"Are you...?" I trailed off, staring at her. What had he told her? What had he said had happened to drive me out of here? And did she seriously believe him?

"What happened yesterday, from your point of view?" she asked, smiling at me encouragingly. I half expected her to hand me crayons and colored paper to describe what had gone down, the way she was talking to me. It wasn't helping with my temper. She obviously thought I was capable of pursuing and forming a physical relationship with Dominic, so why was she addressing me like a child? The two things juxtaposed made my skin crawl, and I did my best to quell the anger inside of me before I flipped this table over at the two of them.

"What happened," I took a deep breath, like I was taking a run-up. "We were talking about this band—"

"The Tantrums," Dominic cut in. I blinked at him, incredulous, and continued.

"We were talking about this band and I guess things got quite heated," I explained, daring him to interrupt me again. "And Dominic grabbed me, held on to my arms, and kissed me, and then he tried to put his hand into my pants."

"And what did you do?" Kathleen prompted me.

"I pushed him off, I said no, and I—"

"No, before that," she said, waving her hand. "Sorry, I should have been clearer. What happened before that?"

"I don't follow you."

"When he was kissing you, what did you do?"

"I…." I cast my mind back to the day before, when I had felt his fingers sinking into my skin, hard enough to leave bruises on my memory. I brushed my fingers over my elbow, as though trying to remind myself how it felt, what it had done to me.

"I didn't do anything," I replied, firmly. "I was in shock. I didn't know how to react."

"So, you kissed him back?"

"No, I didn't do anything," I shot back, my voice rising a little, filling the space between us. She held up a hand.

"I'm not accusing you of anything," she said, but this time her voice was harder around the edges. The kid gloves were off. "I just want to get a good idea of what happened here yesterday."

"Well, I didn't know what to do, so I pushed him off—"

"After a while," Dominic interjected again. Kathleen turned to me expectantly, looking for confirmation. I paused for a moment then nodded, conceding.

"Yes, after a while," I admitted. "And then we argued for a little bit—"

"What were you arguing about?" she asked, cocking her head at me expectantly.

"What had just happened," I replied. "And then I left."

"Where did you go?"

"Out," I waved a hand. "I just didn't want to be around him anymore."

"Why didn't you come to us?" she asked, frowning. "You know we like to deal with these things as quickly and efficiently as we can. If you'd—"

"I didn't want to be *around him* anymore," I shot back. "Like, not in the office. Not anywhere near him."

"Why?" she asked, shaking her head at me again. "I don't follow. You must have known that leaving the office would end up with more…*more* than if you'd just come directly to us to figure this out."

I thought back to the day before again, and even though I knew how I'd felt in that moment, in the second I'd chosen to walk out on to the street, I found myself rewriting my memories. What had once been this grinding wall of discomfort turned into a tantrum; the panic I'd felt replaced by petulance as her version of events permeated mine. If I had just held my shit together, none of this would be happening. If I hadn't let him get to me—

No. No. I shook my head, refusing to hear it. I wasn't going to let her talk me backwards into believing that I was the one who fucked up yesterday.

"I was really upset about what had happened," I explained as best I could, trying to find a way to put into words my feeling that someone had been trying to claw their way out of my head from the inside out, the feeling that Dominic had drawn from me as soon as he'd put his hands on me the day before. "I needed some time to think about what I wanted to do. I appreciate that I shouldn't have left, but I was extremely distressed and I needed some time to—"

"You didn't seem upset," Dominic remarked. "You seemed mad."

I widened my eyes at him, telling him to shut the fuck up, but it wasn't like it mattered. It wasn't like anyone was listening to me.

"Why do you say that, Dominic?" Kathleen asked, turning to him and frowning slightly, that furrow between her brow deepening. I wanted to scream. *Don't listen to him. He's the one who did this to me.*

"She was yelling at me," he said. At least he had the decency to look marginally sheepish, but it wasn't enough. "She…kind of chewed me out. Which I deserved, I guess."

"Yeah, you did," I snarled, my voice catching at the back of my throat and sounding like a bubbling sob. I cursed myself for sounding so pathetic. That was just what I needed to seem even more irrational than he had been making me out to be.

"So, if you were able to express your unhappiness with Dominic to him, why couldn't you come and discuss it with us?" Kathleen asked. I stared at her for a moment because, for a split second, I didn't have an answer. She was right—I could have gone to her. If I could effectively chew him out, I could have kept those words fresh in my mind and marched straight down to HR and spewed it all out to them again. But I didn't. And because she was so obviously right, I couldn't explain to her why she was wrong.

It was one thing to tell him off for that, to be so filled with anger and disgust at him and myself that it overwhelmed the bad feelings for a second. But it was another to sit here opposite her and pretend like this hadn't ripped away another part of me, peeled away another layer and left me raw and stinging like salt water on a wound. Death by a thousand hands on my ass.

How could she not know? She blinked back at me with those bright eyes, expectant, and I wondered if she had never been through something like this before. Never had someone lay hands on her when she didn't want them to. I mean, it was theoretically possible, but she'd have been the first woman I'd ever met who hadn't been. Why couldn't she understand? I silently appealed to some part of her that I knew was there, but was acting like it was either uninterested or non-existent. It didn't do any good.

"I couldn't," I replied, shaking my head uselessly. "I just...couldn't."

"I'm sorry, but we're going to have to discipline you for this," Kathleen explained briskly, crossing and uncrossing her arms as though aware of how matronly it made her look in combination with what she was saying. "I understand that Dominic acted in a way you didn't like—"

"He tried to grope me!" I protested. "How are you not taking this out on him?"

"We're not taking this out on anyone," she replied, infuriatingly. "We just need you to understand that your reaction is not the one we expect from the professionals we employ here—"

"Oh, fuck off," I snapped, the words out before I could stop them. To my surprise, Kathleen actually fell abruptly silent; I had half-assumed that her monotone drone about appropriate behavior was impenetrable, but apparently not.

"Edie," she spoke again, sounding more and more like an irate elementary school teacher with every word that came out of her mouth. "I understand that you're—"

"No, you don't," I replied, hooking my bag up and over my shoulder. "You don't understand much about me, Kathleen. I quit."

"Edie, what the fuck are you doing?" Dominic's face paled and he took a step towards me, reaching out to try and catch me. "We can work this out. I know I was—"

"I don't want any of this anymore," I said, looking between the both of them. "Sorry, I'm done. I'm out of here."

And with that, I turned and marched out of the office, just about keeping my composure until I made it outside. That's when the hot ball of anger that had risen in my chest burst and broke and bubbled up out of me in a gasping sob.

I pulled my phone from my pocket, just like I had done the day before, but this time it wasn't Philip that I wanted to talk to; no, I had someone else in mind, even though I knew that I was the last person she'd expect to hear from right now. But she was the only one who'd been here, and what I needed more than anything was someone who'd been here, someone who knew how this all felt. I couldn't bear to stare back into the eyes of someone like Kathleen who didn't understand any of this. I needed a kindred spirit. I pulled her number up, paused for a moment, and then dialed. She picked up after a couple of rings, and I didn't give her time to speak before the words came tumbling out of my mouth.

"Lena?" My voice sounded hollow, like someone had gouged something out of me. "Can I come over?"

Chapter Thirteen

I HADN'T VISITED LENA'S APARTMENT more than a couple of times before that. I hadn't had a reason to. She was the kind of friend that I invoked only when I needed someone who would say yes when I suggested hitting the club at one in the morning after too many rum-based cocktails. I think I had stopped in here once in the last year, and that was to pick up a dress that I had loaned her the week before. It was a beautiful apartment, one that she shared with her long-time boyfriend Tom, covered in trinkets and carefully coordinated golds and reds and pale woods. As I sat on her couch, my legs tucked up underneath me, the light poured in from an enormous window opposite me, the flickers of sunlight making me blink. She was making tea, chai something, and I felt like the couch was going to swallow me whole.

It was like she had sensed what I needed as soon as I had called her, and she invited me down straightaway—she was out of a job for the time being, something that I hadn't known until I'd made that phone call, or maybe had known distantly but not enough to commit it to memory, maybe she had told me the last time she'd seen me, or maybe Jeannie…

My head kept going down these stupid little corridors of memory, trying to avoid looking head-on at the fact that I'd just quit my job over my stupid inability to deal with my bullshit. I flexed my fingers, looking down at the way the knuckles whitened beneath my skin. What the fuck was I doing here? I should be at work. I should just go back there and tell them that I made a huge mistake and that I wanted my job back and that we could just drop everything and pretend none of this had happened and hey, wasn't Dominic just making a joke with all that stuff anyway?

"Here you go," Lena handed me a mug and I took it, inhaling the syrupy, spicy scent in the hopes that it would bring me back down to earth. She sat down in the large wicker chair opposite me, tucking her feet up underneath her and pulling a blanket across her knees, carefully tucking it in around her as though bolstering herself for what was about to come.

"So…what, uh, what are you here for?" she asked. It might have sounded harsh but I knew that it was a perfectly reasonable question. We didn't do shit like this. In any other situation, I would have gone to Jeannie, gotten drunk, and spent most of the day talking shit and ripping the piss out of each other. But I needed something different. I needed someone who'd been there.

"I…" I fell silent and pressed my lips together. How many times had my friends told me, or had I told my friends, that we would be there for each other no matter what? How many times had someone clasped my hand and looked into my eyes and said "Seriously, any time of the day or night, you just call"? Now that I had actually done that, I couldn't shake this feeling that I was taking advantage. Those words were just platitudes, and I had violated some inbuilt social contact by actually treating them as real.

But I was sitting here in Lena's living room after calling her up in a panic, and I knew that getting up and leaving would somehow be more brutally uncomfortable than having this conversation with her. So, I took a deep breath, another one, and finally said what I needed to say.

"Lena," I began. I could manage her name. That was the start I needed. Words. Come on. I could do words.

"What was it like?" I blurted out at last. "Not…it, not the actual event itself, but…afterwards? What was it like?"

She stared at me for a moment, and I really thought in that second that she was going to get to her feet, pry the cup of tea from my hands, and point me to the door. A strand of hair slipped from the careful bun at the top of her head, and she swiped it back behind her ear, as though angry that it had dared show itself. The silence in the room felt like pain—a pain both of us shared, that both of us were unable to get away from, no matter how hard we tried.

"I didn't even realize that it had happened, at first," she sighed, the words breathy but curiously devoid of tone, as though she was telling a story about someone else entirely. "I mean, I didn't even think something bad had happened. It just…it just went down, and then I left the next day, and he was acting as normal, so I thought, *oh, it must just be how that happens, then.* I really didn't think there was anything wrong with him or what he did for the longest time. Like, a few years, easily."

"If you don't want to talk about this," I assured her, "you don't—"

"You know, I never talked to anyone about this properly," she said, shaking her head and cutting me off. But the way she said it made me wonder if she'd heard the words come out of my mouth at all. She had this faraway look on her face, like she had retreated into memories that she had done her best to bury until now.

"I never thought…I never wanted people to see me like that, you know? Damaged goods," she said, waving a hand. "Or a victim. The way people look at you when they find out, you don't get over that. It changes you forever. It's the first thing people think of…"

She trailed off and shook her head, as though snapping herself back to reality.

"Sorry," she mumbled, a little sheepish. "That's not helpful."

"No, it is," I assured her. "I want to hear—fuck, I want to hear the truth, Lena. You're, what, ten years ahead of me on this? You know more than I do about all of this, I need your inside scoop."

"You know the weirdest part?" she asked, as she leaned forward and frowned. "I don't think it's the worst thing that ever happened to me."

"What do you mean?"

"I just…" She trailed off, sighed, ran her fingers through her hair, started again. "Whenever I spoke to people about it, they were always so horrified, like, they talked about it in these hushed tones like I might snap and break down if I had to face up to it again. There were some nights, don't get me wrong, there were some nights when I would just lie awake and stare at the ceiling and wonder if I would ever get out from under the weight of it. But I never—it fucking sucked, don't get me wrong, and I think the guy who did it is a total piece of shit and it did screw me up for a while knowing that someone could do that to me. But it just didn't…matter that much? In the grand scheme of my life?"

I stayed silent, not knowing how to respond to that, and she hurried in to continue, to justify herself.

"I just felt like whenever people talked to me about rape or getting raped or—or any of it, or when I saw women who had been raped on TV or in movies and stuff, it was always…the worst thing that ever happened to them? It completely changed the course of their lives, like nothing could ever be the same after it happened. And I think that's true for some people, sure, but it just wasn't for me, and it made me feel like I was lying or making it up or something."

I kept my mouth shut.

"I had this—there was a period of time after I realized what had happened where I felt really fucking awful, and a few times I had these flashbacks and it felt as though, *okay, yeah, so this is going to ruin the rest of my life and I just need to get on board with it and accept it,*" she went on. "And I cried a lot and I was really fucking mad at every man who came into my life, because every single one of them was a representation of the guy who'd done that to me and I knew I could never take him to court over it or make him pay. But it…faded, over time. I still think of it sometimes and I still get pissed that he's out there, and sometimes I wonder if I should have called him on it or tried to take him to court or something in case it happened to other women. But I knew that he would never admit to it and besides, what evidence did I have against him anyway?"

The words came tumbling out of her mouth, a stream of consciousness, like she'd been waiting to say all this to someone for years. I could only sit there and try to take it all in, try to make sense of everything she was giving me. But somewhere in there I found something to cling on to. It felt like wrapping my arms around a tree branch in a storm, flimsy and desperate, but maybe just enough to get me through.

"And now I guess it's just something that happened to me," she finished off, a little breathless. It's fucking…I mean, I hate him and I always will, and I hate that this kind of shit happens so often, but for me it just sort of…is?"

"So, you got over it?" I asked. I needed her to say yes.

"No," she said, shaking her head. "It still fucks me up sometimes. But it's more anger than hurt, you know?

Knowing that he got away with it and probably doesn't even realize he did anything wrong."

My shoulders sagged, and I guess she noticed it.

"I'm sorry," she murmured, reaching over to squeeze my hand—she was touchy-feely, always had been, and I tried not to snatch my hand away in petulance that she hadn't given me the answer I'd been hoping for. It wasn't her fault. It wasn't anyone's fault.

"But it does get better," she promised me, her eyes scanning my face desperately for some kind of reaction, some kind of response. "Edie? Hello?"

I lifted my gaze to meet hers and ached when I saw the way she was looking at me.

"I'm sorry," I said, getting to my feet and jolting the tea that I had placed down on the small table in front of me. "I shouldn't have come here. This wasn't fair to do to you—"

"No, sit down," she ordered, her voice firm. "What happened? Before you came here?"

I looked down at her and realized, with a sinking sensation, that I was going to have to talk about this one way or another. Might as well figure out how to do it now. I sat down again, this time perched on the edge of the couch, like I might leap up and make a break for the window at any moment. If it hadn't been a two-story drop down to the street below, I just might have done it.

"I quit my job." I lifted my hands in the air and raised my eyebrows, like I was delivering great news, but my voice was hollow and raw. It still didn't feel real, the truth of the situation still circling somewhere around the outside of my brain, distant and blurred. But those words threw it for a second into sharp relief, and I felt panic seize my chest

"What?" Lena gasped. "What do you mean?"

"I mean, the guy I work with, my partner—well, my ex-partner now—he tried to make out with me and feel me up in the office yesterday and I walked out and now they're taking his side over it, so I just quit," I blurted out before I had a chance to tamper with my thoughts. Lena blinked at me a couple of times, clearly trying to make sense of everything she'd just heard. I didn't blame her. It was...a lot. Considering that our conversations hadn't gone a lot deeper than swapping clothes before this had all come up, doubly so.

"Wait, hold up," she lifted a hand. "What did you say he did? This partner guy?"

"Dominic," I sighed. "He...we were arguing yesterday, and he suddenly just went to kiss me."

"Jesus Christ," she snapped, her voice taking on a sudden harsh edge that made me jump even though I knew it wasn't aimed at me. "Fucking *men*. Let me guess, you were showing any kind of emotion at all so he took that to mean that it must translate into you wanting the dick?"

I snorted with laughter, but there wasn't any mirth in it. I nodded.

"I guess so," I replied.

"Did you? Want him, I mean?"

"Oh, fuck no." I shook my head. "I just...fuck, it just scared the shit out of me, you know? I was so worried that it was going to happen again."

"Not every guy is out to rape you," she pointed out bluntly, and even though I knew she was right, I shook my head.

"I can't tell the difference between the ones that are and the ones that aren't," I replied, and we both fell silent for a second before I spoke again. "I don't think I can have sex," I continued, figuring that the floodgates had opened now and I might as well take advantage of them.

Lena shook her head. "No, it'll happen again, I know it seems tough now, but—"

"No, I mean, I don't think I'm able to physically have sex anymore," I interrupted her. "I was with this guy—this really fucking great guy—a couple of days ago, and we were fooling around and when he went to fuck me…"

I trailed off again, the memory of the pain ugly and heavy in my mind. But I took a deep breath and forced myself to keep talking. I was already feeling that odd, light, out-of-body sensation I had when I was sharing too much with someone I didn't know well enough, and even though I knew I would regret this later, it was addictive in the moment.

"It just really fucking hurt," I finished up. "We tried a few times, but it was like someone had nailed up wood over me or something. It just wasn't happening."

Lena fell silent, a furrow appearing in her brow, as she processed what I'd said.

"Did that kind of thing happen to you as well?" I asked, and she shook her head.

"No, not…after, but before I was raped I did," she replied slowly. "Really bad pain? Like you couldn't take anything inside you?"

"Yeah," I nodded. "It was like losing five virginities at once."

She giggled, and I managed to crack a smile at last.

"Five?"

"Maybe six."

"You know, I honestly didn't have any of that after the… after it happened," she said, avoiding using the word again. I felt a jolt of recognition as I realized I did the same thing. Even now, a decade after it had happened to her, she could still get overwhelmed and needed to duck from calling it what it was. I knew that feeling, that the power of the word was too much to speak so many times in a row.

"But it seems like it would be a normal reaction," she shrugged. "You should talk to a doctor about it. I really don't know. It cleared up for me on its own after a while, but I think some of it was just…brute force, to be honest. Like, I didn't let myself *not* do it, you know? I just…forced myself through it, until I could do it again."

"That sounds pretty grim," I winced, remembering the savagery of that pain that had torn through me before.

"Yeah, it probably wasn't the way I should have dealt with it," she replied. "You're going to therapy, right?"

"I went once, but I haven't gone back since," I admitted. "It helped a little, but it just seemed like a lot to take on."

"It is," she said. "At least, it was for me. But it really, really helped me get a handle on all of it, and it's better to start sooner rather than later, before all the bad patterns of thought get a foothold in your head."

Something flickered over her face. Maybe it was pain or fear or sadness, but it was enough to snap me to my senses.

"Oh, Jesus, Lena." I picked up my tea and put it down again, not knowing what to do with my hands. "I'm so sorry I dragged this all up for you. It's not fair—"

"No, don't be stupid," she shook her head, her voice a little harsh, though it felt more aimed at herself than me. "If I can stop you from going through what I have had to, then I will."

"But it's not fair," I persisted impotently. "You still had to go through it all, and now I'm here—"

"Now you're here looking for a way to avoid dragging yourself through the sea of shit that I had to deal with after it happened," she shot back. "It might not have been the worst thing that ever happened to me, but it fucked me up for a while. It's probably going to fuck you up for a while, too. Anything I can do to help with that, I'll do. And I'm sorry, but you're just going to have to sit there and listen."

She met my gaze, and her eyes were flashing with something sharper-edged than before. I let out a long breath, my head sagging down to my chest. I picked up my tea and took a sip, and even though it was still a little too hot to drink, I savoured it.

"Thank you for this," I managed. "For all of it."

"You'd do the same for me," she replied simply. And she was right. Dead right. It was with a grim inevitability that I accepted the fact that, at some point, I was probably going to have to guide someone else through everything that I was going through—this would happen to someone I loved, or it had already happened and they had just done their best to ignore it till now and soon it would come bubbling up and over. But I would be there, like Lena had been for me. Just as soon as I was out of the woods.

Chapter Fourteen

"OW, FUCK, OW OW, FUCKING *OW*."

I knew that yelping into the quiet of my apartment wasn't going to make anything easier, but damned if it didn't feel like it did. I tossed the dilator angrily to the side of the bed and glared at it, the stupid pink plastic glistening with the medicated lubricant in the light of the candle I'd lit in an attempt to set the mood. I could almost remember a time when spending time with a plastic dick and my hand between my legs was a fun evening, not one that made me seize up with stress at the very thought of it.

Vaginismus. That was the name they'd given me for this stupid fucking affliction: that feeling like someone had clamped my legs together. I had had to visit my gynaecologist and they had stuck a cotton swab up me to check that it wasn't just some kind of infection, and as soon as I felt the thing moving inside me I felt as though I was going to faint with the pain. I swallowed heavily and focused all my attention on the odd grey damp spot on the ceiling above me, wondering if they'd somehow swapped out the cotton swab I'd seen them holding with several kitchen knives when I hadn't been looking. That's sure as hell what it felt like.

"So, what do I do about it?" I asked, my legs wound around each other twice like I was pulling up a drawbridge around my vagina.

"Uh..." The doctor, who seemed about as confused as I was about this, consulted her computer again, frowning at the screen. I saw the word on it there again, and tried to say it in my head—I tumbled over the vowels and the consonants and came up blank.

"So, it's a chronic pain condition," the doctor explained slowly, nodding as though she was just remembering all of this herself. "And it's...the best course of action is to take foreplay really slowly and do what you can to stretch out the vagina before penetration."

Since when was "stretch out" a phrase I ever wanted to apply to my pussy? My whole life I had been trying to get myself tighter down there, and now I was stuck trying to go in the other direction. There were no winners in the game of cunts, it seemed.

"You can also buy numbing lubricant," she went on. "Which should—"

"Wait, like, lube so I can't feel anything down there?" I frowned at her. "What's the point of that?"

"You could be penetrated," she said, shifting on her seat. I hated it when she used that word, almost as much as she seemed to hate using it. Every time she said it I had the image of a pen pushing through a piece of paper, puncturing the pure white page.

"Yeah, but I couldn't *feel* it," I pointed out again. "Why would I want to do that?"

"Some women..." She trailed off again. Jesus, this woman talked about vaginas for a living, was mine really that abnormal that she was rendered speechless in the face of it? Did vaginas even have faces? Anyway.

"Some women would rather just be able to take penetration than anything else," she finished up, attempting diplomacy. I stared at her for a moment. So, some of the be-vagina'd among us would honestly rather feel nothing and be able to take a dick than to let down the dick-havers in their life? I thought back to Philip in my bed, frustrated but doing his best to understand the first time this happened, and thanked God I'd found someone who didn't want me to anesthetize myself so he could put his dick in me.

"Are there any other options?" I sighed. "Ones that don't involve a partner?"

"Have you ever heard of dilators before?"

Dilators. Such an ugly, clinical word—I couldn't even get them from my doctor's office or a drug store, I had to order a kit online and wait for it to arrive at my door. I had opened it while waiting for my morning tea to brew, and found a snazzy purple clip-on carry case that fourteen-year-old me would have been very proud to keep her lip glosses in. Except it wasn't mango-scented sparkly balm in there—it was four Russian nesting dildoes, varying in size and neatly nested inside each other, and all in this garish shade of pastel pink. I didn't know what color I'd been expecting them to be, but this shade was somewhere between "children's toy" and "doctor's office" and all that made me think of was kids with cancer. Not exactly words that got me going. But at least they were here now, and I could go about fixing my stupid, broken vagina.

It wasn't like I had a lot to spend my time on these days anyway, what with having quit my job and all. Because somehow that had actually stuck. I had seriously thought about slinking back in to the office to try and get my job back, but the only thing that really appealed to me about it was having something to do all day long. I didn't actually want to go back there, or work with Dominic again, not as long as I lived. I found myself getting a little cabin-feverish in my apartment—I could have sworn those dilators were looking at me sometimes—but I had been working steadily since I had left college and there was something a little exciting about the new possibilities this opened up. It was terrifying, too, obviously, but exciting. I had no clue what I was going to do next, what I was meant to do, but I would take all of this and run with it and see where I ended up.

But in the meantime, I had a project, and that was getting my goddamn body to do what it was meant to again. It was so strange, because I could remember, I could imagine, how good it had once felt to have something inside me like that. But every time I lay back on the bed with one of those stupid fucking dilators and my knees around my ears and tried to focus on just how good it had once felt, pain tore through my lower body and I was reminded once again that I wasn't going to be able to get away from this with a memory.

"Ugh," I muttered, glaring once more at the dilator that was sitting next to me. This wasn't going to get any easier. If it hadn't been for Philip, I would have given up on this already and committed myself to a life of sanitary pads and external vibrators. But he was still there, a promise to make this all worthwhile, and I couldn't shake how much I wanted to be with him. Properly. The way I was used to.

Not that he had been anything other than the sweetest damn thing about all of this. In fact, he was coming around to visit that evening after running some errands in the city, and part of the reason I was trying so damn hard to get these things up myself was so we could actually have sex. He hadn't been pushing for anything more than what we were doing—which had involved the heaviest of heavy petting so far, basically everything but—but I was the kind of person who took a "you can't do this" as a "watch me try" and I was going to have sex with Philip if it killed me. Which, judging by the burning sensation lancing through my lower body right now, it just might.

I sighed and swept everything off the bed, letting it land on the cluttered floor with a clatter. Throwing a tantrum about this wasn't going to help, but it made me feel momentarily better and as long as those things weren't in my eyeline I wouldn't have to think about the failure that I'd just endured.

I rolled myself out bed, got to my feet, and reached for my underwear so I could get dressed in time for Philip arriving. But now that I had failed again, I felt like a little of the wind had been taken out of my sails. Every time he came around, I found myself wondering if this would be the night, if my post-assault waiting period would be up and I could have painless sex once more, but I still seemed to be stuck in processing. Fuck. *Fuck.*

It wasn't fair, not one bit. I wasn't the one who had gone and done *that* to someone. I shouldn't be the one punished for this. As I tidied my apartment, I found my brain running through the familiar pattern that it had followed a lot in the last few days. I was pretty fucking sure that Kieran wasn't lying in his apartment wondering why he couldn't get it up. His brain probably wasn't filled with those ugly thoughts that came to me when I was trying to get to sleep at nights, the ones that harangued me with questions about *what if* and *maybe if you'd just.* He was probably out living his life somewhere, not aware that he'd had this effect on me—hell, maybe even doing it to other women, too. And even if he had realized, even if he was repentant, he still hadn't bothered to reach out to me to say he was sorry. Neither had Dominic, for that matter— different circumstances, but same continuum; both were men who'd decided they could do what they wanted to my body without checking in with me. Both were men who probably, judging by their reactions, thought that I'd brought it on myself. That I'd wanted it. That I was a liar.

It was hard not to hate men, sometimes. Not all men—well, not Philip, at least—but I would walk down the street and look around and wonder how many of those men had made someone feel the way I did. My therapist assured me this was normal, that it was just projection after what had happened to me and that as long as I was unable or unwilling to pursue some kind of retribution against Kieran for his actions, I would transfer the anger and helplessness I felt in the face of what he'd done onto men who hadn't done a thing to me, to the representations of him that I saw all around me. But when I thought about it—when I thought about me, and Lena, and the looks on the faces of my friends when I'd been groped and they'd all but "what did you expect?"-ed me—it was hard to keep the fury in me from bubbling over. It hurt knowing that this was a given, knowing that we had come to expect it. Sometimes, it felt impossible. I knew it would fade, because those thoughts had only just found form in my head, but for the time being, they felt wedged there uncomfortably. The upside was that at least I didn't get catcalled at much with a foul look on my face.

I finished tidying up, Max trundling around my feet the whole time and trying to trip me up, and put on a pair of pants before Philip arrived. I knew I could have just lazed around with nothing on my bottom half—he certainly wouldn't have complained—but it was a reminder of the stupid failure I'd just struggled through.

There was a knock at the door and I went to answer it, a little uptick in my chest bringing a smile to my face despite myself. It was strange, to have this mess of feelings in my head—to deal with that jagged-edged horror nightmare in one half on my brain and to be all sparkly, fluffy, pink romantic comedy in the other. I had thought that getting over all of this would be a continuous full-on existential mind journey, but I still had to buy cat food and clean the dishes and go on dates in between those parts. The banality was comforting in a way that I had never known it could be.

"Hey," I beamed when I pulled the door open. Philip was waiting there on the other side for me, and he leaned over the threshold and kissed me on the mouth. He tasted of sweet mint, like he'd been chewing gum before he'd come out. He always did when he came around here, and I thought it was exceedingly cute that he still cared about how his breath smelled, especially when I had the temerity to kiss him when I'd just woken up in the morning.

"Hey," he replied as he pulled away, and he stepped over the threshold and pulled me properly into his arms. There was still something about the feel of his arms around me, stronger than I would have thought from just looking at him, that wiped the memory of my earlier failures from my head. When I was with him, I wasn't thinking about the fact that I'd quit my job with meager savings and nothing new to go to. I wasn't thinking about how my body had decided to stop cooperating with me. I wasn't thinking about the fact that I had woken up that morning, swung my legs out of bed, and put my feet straight into a pile of cat vomit that Max had left there at some point overnight. I was just thinking about us and the way we felt together, and it felt like a relief to have those other thoughts lifted from my head for a while.

"How's it going?" I asked as I pressed my head into his chest, inhaling his scent deeply. My voice was a little muffled but that wasn't going to get me to pull away from him. "Did you get everything you needed done?"

"Yeah, pretty much," Philip replied, ducking down so that he could greet Max as the cat came tumbling towards him excitedly. Sometimes I wondered if Max liked Philip better than he liked me, and my fears were hardly assuaged watching the way that Mx barged his head into Philip's hand. I bet he wouldn't have thrown up at the side of the bed had Philip been there.

"What do you want to do today?" he asked, straightening up again and smiling at me. I shifted my weight from hip to hip, stalling—I wanted to go out and do something, but I was being careful with my savings and I didn't want to spend cash on stuff that I wasn't certain I could afford until I had a new job. I had enough to keep me in rent, cat food, and ramen for the next six months, but I had always been unendingly careful with my money and I wasn't going to waste it on shit I wasn't certain I needed. I knew he would offer to pay and that he would mean it when he said he didn't mind, but I didn't like adding up how much he'd spent on me in the last couple of weeks since my job had ended.

"Uh, how about we stay in and watch a movie and cook something?" I suggested hurriedly. "I found this new recipe that I want to try..."

I trailed off unconvincingly, and he eyed me for a moment, clearly not buying what I was trying to sell.

"I mean, I'm not going to say no to hanging around here all evening with you and the cat, but I really don't mind covering for a bit if you want to go out—"

"No, you've paid for the last half-dozen things," I reminded him, slumping back against the bathroom doorframe behind me. "I don't want you to think I'm just using you..."

"What? For cat-babysitting?" he teased. Then, seeming to sense that this was really bothering me, he stepped forward and cupped my face in his hand.

"Hey, really, it's cool," he promised with a smile. I couldn't help but return it; there was something about his smile that made my heart sing. "I know as soon as you get a job you're going to be paying me back. Don't worry about it."

"I just hate that I had to meet you when everything in my life is a fucking wreck," I said, shaking my head and feeling irritated at myself for the obvious reasons, but even more irritated at myself for bringing it up around him. We were early enough into the relationship that I would have preferred it if I could keep up the pretence of me being this effortless, brilliant, elegant power-woman with everything in her life in hand and under control.

"It's not," he said, cocking his head at me, and I could see the tiniest flicker of frustration pass over his face once more. "Things are just changing, that's all. You'll get used to it."

"You're right," I said. I furrowed my brow at him, shaking my head. "Sorry for being such a brat."

"You'll just have to make it up to me later," he said, flashing me a dirty smile, the kind that would have gotten him arrested for indecent behavior in public. I giggled.

"Not in front of the cat," I teased, and let my shoulders sink down as the pressure lifted from me.

"Hi," he greeted me again, now that the air had cleared.

"Hi," I replied, and stepped towards him and slipped my arms around his shoulders and kissed him, and this time there was nothing sweet about it. I could still taste that mint on his breath, but I hardly had time to linger on it as he pushed his tongue into my mouth and began to kiss me harder. His hands came to my waist, and he guided me in the direction of the bedroom, and I did my best to shut down the panicked little voice in the back of my head that was determined to remind me of my failure just an hour or so ago. I sank my fingers into his shoulders, forcing myself to focus on the sensations, the feel of his breath hot on my skin as he kissed that spot right where my ear met my neck. My bare toes curled against the floor as his hands slid over my back, keeping me steady, before he slowly lowered me down onto the bed.

"I missed you," I murmured as he moved on top of me, leaning down to kiss me again. He smiled and held back for just a moment before he went in once more.

"I missed you, too," he replied, his voice heavier than before, as though weighed down by desire. I knew how he felt; no matter how many times we came together like this, it never got old. We made out on that bed like teenagers for God knows how long, until I could feel his cock straining against his jeans, hard on my hip. One of the only good things about not being able to *do* it was that everything else slowed down as a consequence. I hooked my ankles behind his back and pressed myself against him, finding some relief in the hardness of him against me, but I needed more. And he was more than willing to deliver.

He undressed me quickly, deftly, pulling my shirt over my head and quickly undoing my jeans and pulling them down my body until I was in nothing but a pair of panties. He looked up at me, flashing me a smile before he began to work his way from the twist of my ankle right up to the inside of my thigh, brushing kisses against my skin, the pleasure heightening with every touch until I was wriggling needily beneath him. He always made me wait like this, and sometimes it felt sweet—pushing my boundaries to see how much I could take before I'd crack, something playful and lightly teasing. Other times, like today, it felt like straight-out torture, watching his mouth work closer and closer to my pussy until I felt as though I was a dam waiting to burst.

Finally, he reached the inside of my thigh, planting one soft, warm kiss against the crook of my leg before he moved to press his lips against my panties. I inhaled sharply at the feel of his hot mouth against my skin, even with the barrier of my underwear between us; he looked up at me again as I lifted my hips to grind against him slightly, and something about the flash of satisfaction in his eyes was enough to tell me that he was nearly ready to make me come. I knew he liked it when I was a little desperate, and I was more than a little right now. Finally, he hooked his fingers around my panties and pulled them down, letting his fingers trace a line down my legs as he went. I tipped my head back and let out a little moan of anticipation, already desperate for what I knew was coming next.

He slid back between my legs once he had gotten rid of my panties, tucking his hands beneath my ass and pulling me closer to him. He looked down at me—really looked, as though savouring the sight of me—and then leaned down and finally, finally, pressed his mouth against my pussy.

I wasn't sure exactly what you'd call the noise that I made—if there was even a name for it—but I couldn't give a damn how I sounded or about anything else in that moment. With so many of the other guys I'd been with, I'd felt this urge to censor myself when we were having sex, to make sure that they were only seeing specific parts of me and that those specific parts were as perfect as they could be, like they might storm out in a fury if my stomach curved outward for a second or if my thighs spread when they rested on the bed. But I never felt that way with Philip. Maybe it was because my body had already betrayed both of us in a way I could never have predicted, but I just didn't have the same defenses up with him. As he flattened his tongue against my clit, his hands moved across my body, across my distinctly unflat stomach and my slightly uneven boobs and my ass that was more fleshy than thick, and I couldn't think about anything but how good it felt.

He moved with slow strokes at first, taking his time and seeming to savour the moment, his tongue soft against my clit as his fingers settled on my ass, sinking into my flesh. I closed my eyes and reached down to rake my fingers through his hair. Another thing, too, was that I never felt the urge to writhe around and fake the absurd heights of pleasure that I had with other guys, because I knew he could actually make me come. That was a nice change.

When this was the main event, he didn't seem as invested in rushing through it to get to the good stuff as my other partners had, and for once, I was able to relax and actually enjoy getting oral instead of vanishing inside my own brain as I tried to keep my body looking nice and my moans sounding genuine and shit, was I taking too long? Was he getting bored? With Philip, I could just lose myself to the moment, to how good his soft mouth felt on me, to the oxymoronic roughness of his stubble against the inside of my thighs. He sealed his lips around my clit and focused in his attention, sucking lightly as he flicked his tongue against me, sending jolts of pleasure through my entire body. I found a smile had broken out across my face as I gave in to the sensations, my fingers tensing in his hair. How had I forgotten how good it felt to just have someone go down on me? Before Philip, it had always been a race to the main event, a "no, I'm as generous a lover as I said I was in my profile, see" tick-box. But this, this was something different. Special.

"Fuck!" I was pulled out of all that romanticising as he let out a soft moan against me, sending shudders of pleasure up through my entire body. Shifting his head a little, he paid some attention to my labia, drawing them gently and one at a time into his mouth and sucking lightly. My toes curled. *Fuck.* That felt good.

He began to move his hands across my body again, but instead of feeling like a distraction, the sensations just crowded in on top of each other until I couldn't take any more—my brain was consumed by it, my body aching for some relief, and as soon as he returned his attention to my clit once more, I felt myself arcing with pleasure, edging closer. He drew me into his mouth once more, sucking harder this time, his fingers grazing deftly across my nipples and drawing them to hardness too. My brow furrowed and I pressed my lips together and I focused in on the feeling, just the feeling of it—

When I came, it felt as though someone had struck a match against my skin and sent the flame racing through me. The orgasm radiated out from my center to take control of every inch of my body for just a moment, a giggle escaping my lips as the euphoria made me a little giddy for a moment or two, and then receded; I leaned down, pushing his head back from my pussy and kissing him hard, tasting myself on him and craving more. Craving *it*. For a moment, that crucial moment, I could imagine how good it would feel to have him inside me. I clung to it, and I dived into my bedside dresser and fumbled in the drawer for a condom.

"What are you doing?" he asked, his breath still coming a little quicker than normal and his mouth glistening with my wetness.

"Fuck me," I panted, finally finding a condom and pressing it into his hand. "Please. I want you too. I'm ready."

"Are you sure?" He frowned at me for a moment. We hadn't tried since the first time, when it had all gone so wrong, and I could see why he might have been nervous about giving it another shot—but I needed to try right now before I had a chance to let the panic sneak up on me once more. I nodded and lay back on the bed, excitement carrying me through, looking up at the ceiling.

"Yeah, I'm sure," I grinned, and watched as he quickly undressed and sheathed himself. I felt bad about not returning the foreplay favor, but this was better, this was what I wanted to give him. I didn't want to wait, couldn't wait, knew that the bad feelings would have time to catch up on me if I didn't go for this right then and there. He leaned down to kiss me and parted my legs, and I hooked my ankles behind him as I had done earlier and pulled him in close to me. I felt him press up against the entrance to my pussy, and then—

Pain. That familiar pain. It wasn't the kind of pain you could breathe through until it all went away; it wasn't the kind of pain you could pretend you weren't feeling. Raw, burning agony that made me draw away from him on instinct. It was something deep inside me, a natural reaction that went *ow, no* as soon as he tried to penetrate me. How could I have been so stupid? The pain brought me crashing straight back down to earth once more, reminding me of just how rough this was, that it wasn't going to be fixed by true love's kiss.

"Edie?" Philip asked, his brow creased, and I tried to sit with it for a moment longer before I shook my head and pulled away from him. I felt tears prick my eyes, partly because of the pain and partly because of the humiliation. This wasn't *fair.* I just wanted to have sex with this awesome guy I was dating, and my body was practically nailing doors shut in response. How many shitty men had I had sex with over the years, and this was the one my vagina said no to? How did this happen?

"It's okay," he assured me, but I could hear the tension in his voice; I knew what he was thinking, that if we'd just stuck to our usual playtime, we would have been better off and I wouldn't have been lying here aching between my legs and feeling like an idiot for not being able to get my body to damn work.

"It's not," I shot back, knowing I was acting like a child but needing to indulge my anger for a second. "I've been working so hard with the dilators now, for a month!"

"Yeah, but they said it doesn't just clear up like that," he reminded me. "It takes time."

I pulled the covers over myself, not wanting to look at my naked body and be reminded of what I had just failed to do. He sighed and ran his fingers through his hair, pulling off the condom and dumping it in the trash can next to my bed. He reached over to touch my hip; I wanted to pull away, but I didn't have the energy, so I just lay there, letting all those ugly thoughts begin to wash away.

"You know I'm not doing this because of you, right?" I lifted my head and looked at him, and tried to remember how many times I'd started conversations off like this in the last few weeks. He rolled his eyes skyward.

"I know that," he replied firmly, his voice tense and restrained, like he was trying to keep from snapping at me. "You know I know that, Edie."

"I'm sorry, I just..." I trailed off, twisting my head so I could bury my face in the pillow for a moment before I forced myself back upright to look him in the eye. "I just feel like I'm broken and I'm dragging you along with my brokenness and it doesn't feel fair because I don't know if I'll ever be normal again."

"Well, I never knew you as normal," he pointed out.

"Oh, thanks, that makes me feel a bunch better," I looked up at him, raising my eyebrows as playfully as I could manage, and he waved his hand at me.

"You know what I mean," he replied, patient. "This is just...this is just how I've always known you. And it's fine. It's good, even."

"I just don't think it's fair that I could have proper sex with other guys, and—"

"This is enough for me," he cut me off again, firmly. "And forgive me if I don't particularly want to hear about what you got up to before me, alright?"

"Alright," I sighed, looking up to meet his gaze. I managed a smile at last, even though it felt a little rictus. "Thank you for being so understanding about this. I promise I'm working on it. It will get better eventually."

"So, until then I'll just have to get in plenty of practice with everything else," he said, cocking his head at me and raising his eyebrows, his eyes travelling lewdly down my body. I giggled, and he pulled me into his lap and kissed me again and the pain between my legs—not to mention the one in my head—finally start to recede again.

Chapter Fifteen

"I'M SORRY, WHAT?"

I was sitting at the breakfast bar in my apartment, in a pair of underwear and a huge shirt I'd stolen from Philip a few days before. I leaned down absently and pressed my nose into the fabric, inhaling his smell, and letting the scent of him soothe me a little because this phone call had me all kinds of bothered. I hadn't expected to hear from any of the bands I'd worked with again, let alone The Tantrums, let alone now.

"We just wanted to check to see if it was true," Katie's voice came down the line, crisp and clear and in control. A tiny part of me was proud of her; I had worked in this industry probably longer than she had, and it was harder than people let on to get to a point where you stopped taking shit and started standing up for yourself. And, judging by the fact that she was reaching out to me to confirm for herself what had happened, she had grown tired of shoveling manure herself. It took me till someone tried to stick their hand down my pants, but I was glad she'd gotten there quicker than I had.

"Yeah, it's true," I confirmed, with a frown forming unbidden on my face. She had called to ask whether or not I'd really quit work at the label. I wasn't sure why she seemed to give a damn but I wasn't going to hang up on her. I had an inkling, just the tiniest one, that she might actually be on my side in this and right now I would take support from anyone. Outside of Philip and Jeannie, I was pretty certain that everyone else around me thought I had made a big-ass fucking mistake by quitting the label and I didn't have it in me to contradict them. Finding work in this business was tough, and doubly so when you quit your last job for reasons that you couldn't exactly go into in a job interview without using the word "underwear."

"Why did you leave?" she went on, and I could hear some conferring in the background; the rest of the band were there, no doubt, and I took a deep breath and plucked up the courage to tell the truth. If they were thinking about working with Dominic, they needed to know what he was really like.

"Uh, Dominic, my partner, he tried to…he tried to kiss me and other stuff when I didn't want it," I replied, feeling histrionic for even bringing it up, even though she had asked. I always felt uncomfortable when I had to talk about it, not just because it put me back in that bad place again, but because I felt like I was waving my arms around and obnoxiously demanding attention. I pinched the bridge of my nose and closed my eyes for a second; my therapist had been very clear that these kind of feelings of guilt and discomfort were normal when it came to talking about stuff like this, but knowing that and living it were two very different things.

"Right," Katie replied slowly, dragging the word out so I could practically hear every letter. She fell silent, but I heard some more conferring at the other end of the line and took a deep breath. I still couldn't figure out what this was about, but I could just be honest and upfront and hope that the universe finally decided to give me something decent in return. I waited for what felt like a quarter-hour as Katie and the band talked in muffled tones, wondering what the hell this was about. It was quarter to ten on a

Tuesday morning and I felt as though I had been whipped straight back into the office with one phone call. I could practically smell that chunky scent of Dominic's cheap, ugly aftershave.

Finally, Katie came back on the line, letting out a long breath that translated to a sweep of static into my ear.

"So, we got offered a contract with your old label," Katie explained quickly, breathlessly. "But we knew—we knew that Dominic had never come to any of our shows and he all but admitted that you were the one pushing for us before you left."

"Oh, did he?" I replied, a smile sneaking up my face. It would have been so like Dominic to try and keep the high ground by pretending like he'd never heard of them and was just doing this on someone else's suggestion; he had this thing about bands he was proved wrong on, always had. And now here they were on the phone with me instead.

"Yeah, and it didn't really sit right with us," she admitted. "We didn't want to work with someone who seemed so ambivalent about our music, you know?"

"Oh, I know," I replied, digging up that memory of Dominic refusing for the dozenth time to listen to them. I wondered who had twisted his arm—someone in the office, someone else he was trying to hook up with? Or maybe he'd just been unable to avoid the hype that was building around them any longer. Someone else would snap them up soon enough if the handful of interviews and album reviews I'd come across over the last few weeks were any indication.

"So, we…uh, we said we didn't want to sign unless you were there," Katie continued, her voice a little shaky. "Do you think you'd consider coming back? For us?"

I fell silent, staring down at Max, who had just finished thoroughly cleaning his paws and was now sitting there staring up at me as he patiently waited for me to remember that it was time to feed him. His eyes were wide and impassive, and mine were wide and a little panicked. This was a lot. A whole lot.

"Did they ask you to make this call?" I asked. I could just imagine Dominic urging them to reach out to me, knowing that if I saw his number on my phone I would likely toss it into the river.

"No, but I wanted to talk to you about it first," she explained. "I wanted you to hear this from us. We know you've been fighting for us for a while and it wouldn't seem right if we signed up with some..."

She trailed off, leaving the word unspoken, but I could tell from the flicker of disdain in her voice that she thought as highly of Dominic as I did. I smirked childishly; *good.* I was glad his snakey routine wasn't working on everyone he ran into.

"Yeah," I confirmed. "I get it."

"So, do you think you could come back?"

"Uh, can I have some time to think about it?" I asked. My brain was already fluttering with panic as I considered the implications of saying no—or of saying yes.

"Of course," she replied smoothly, sounding suddenly like the calm businesswoman I knew she was trying to project. I couldn't help but smile; when I'd met them only a few months before, they'd seemed like a collection of kids from a small town with a big dream, and now here she was making demands to a label that wanted her. I was impressed; she had bigger ovaries than I had at her age.

"Thanks for...thanks for making a case for me, though," I replied awkwardly. "It means a lot."

"Thanks for stanning for us in the first place," she replied, her voice a little gushy.

"Stanning?"

"Sorry, for pushing for us in the first place," she quickly filled in the blanks. "We appreciate it. And if…if you don't end up coming back, then we'd still like to work with you. If possible."

"I'll bear that in mind," I said, wondering what she thought I could do outside the label but still flattered she was saying it. "I'll get back in touch soon."

"Talk later."

I hung up the phone, placing it carefully flat-down on the bar in front of me and staring at the screen as it paused for a moment before going to black once more. I could still hear Katie's voice in my ear, telling me that they were holding out for me, that they would wait for me, like a romance heroine leaning out the window of a train. Hmm. This was interesting. This was *really* interesting.

I wondered what kind of state Dominic had to be in about now; he must have been going flat-out crazy knowing that it was his fault that the label couldn't sign a band who were blowing up. He probably wanted nothing more than to get the ink on those contracts and lock them in before one of the competitors could swoop in and pick them up, but he'd been the one to back me into that corner and force me out. He could have owned what he did and not made me out to be the asshole, but instead he had to defend his own pathetic ass because his stupid fucking ego couldn't take the fact that I didn't want to blow him as soon as I was given the chance. I knew I was acting like a kid, but I couldn't keep the smile from curling up my lips. Fuck him. *Fuck* him. I was glad that he had ended up in this hellish position and I hoped that he knew how much I was enjoying it. I fully expected to get a call from him any moment now, pressing me to make a decision that suited him.

And maybe I could have gone back: this would be my way to take some kind of a stand and let him knew where my limits were without ending up jobless and living on dry cereal for the next three months. It would have been so easy to just pick up the phone, give him a call, savor the chewing-out that I would get to give him, and go back. I could stand in that office again and pick up where I left off, knowing that I could parlay what had happened into a whole lot more influence and respect for a change. If I had a choice, this wouldn't be how I climbed the corporate ladder, but I had to take what I could get. Didn't I?

I scooped Max up in my arms and he sank his claws into my upper arm in protest, the pain bringing me back down to earth with a crash. Sure, I could go back. I could stand on the other side of that desk and fight with him about music, and know that deep in his soul he didn't respect my opinion enough to really give a shit. The Tantrums, I could hear him arguing, were a fluke. He'd still been there longer. He was the one who had more experience here, more practice at this. He was the one who should be in charge. I wanted to scream when I heard his voice in my head again, so accurate in dredging up the shit that he'd said to me in the past that it was almost eerie. This wouldn't change anything. It wouldn't change *enough*. It might mean he kept his hands the fuck to himself unless he was damn sure someone else wanted them, but that didn't mean that I would suddenly step up to take equal partnership in our office. He would still be turning up with EPs by straight white guys who thought their ex-girlfriends were bitches when I was long dead and rotting in my grave.

I buried my face in Max's fur, remembering what I'd named him for when I got him—that Mad Max movie, the one with Charlize Theron. The one where she'd been nothing but a raging badass. She wouldn't have taken any of this shit; she'd have probably torn his dick off with her mechanical hand by now. I grinned for a moment at the thought, however gory. I didn't want to have to face him again. I didn't want to have to see him again in my entire life if I could avoid it. And I could.

I let my shoulders sink. Even though I knew I should have given things a little more thought than that, I knew the decision was made. Alone in that office with him, I would never stop being on my guard; every time he brushed past me, I would probably go for his throat on sheer instinct. It was better for both of us if I didn't go back. I just had to ignore how fucked-up it was that the only way I could convince myself not to go back there was to convince myself that it was the best thing for *him*.

I pulled up my laptop and headed to the job sites that I'd been perusing the last few weeks, hoping this time I might find something a little more suited to what I was going for. I had already put in a few applications for coffee shop positions and bartending work, even though it felt like a step back; I had to remind myself that Jeannie cheerfully worked service jobs all the time and that I should get the fuck off my high horse and accept that I might have to start over somewhere new. But it was difficult, especially when I'd worked so hard to get where I was at the label. I stared at a job post, trying to make sense of the words on the screen in front of me, but they blurred out and squiggled around my brain uselessly. I slammed the laptop shut. This wasn't *fair*. None of this was my fault, and *all* of this was my fault. If I wasn't feeling the financial squeeze brought on by unemployment, I would have called my therapist and gotten an emergency appointment. As it was, I would rather eat dinner that wasn't just noodles for the next week than spend an hour venting to someone when I had a cat right there who was way more affordable. Max glanced up at me from where he'd flopped down on the couch, as though he knew what I was thinking, and his eyes widened nervously. I snorted mirthlessly. Even my damn cat was sick of hearing about my shit.

I looked at my phone, wondering if I should give Philip a call and talk this out with him—or maybe Jeannie—discuss those heavy, nasty thoughts that had implanted themselves in my brain again. But I was bored of talking about this. What about those TV shows that had a trauma arc? The ones where the person would sit there and through tears give a big speech about what had happened and the episode would close on their loved one hugging them and promising to help them through it? I wanted that. I didn't want this sprawling, messy shadow that spread out to fill in every corner of my life. I wanted a fucking break from this. I wanted it to be over. What these guys had done to me had fucked up my career, my sex life, my ability to fucking trust myself and the way I felt because I was so sure that all of it was somehow influenced by what had happened. It wasn't fair. It wasn't *fair.*

I got to my feet and marched through to my bedroom, certain for a moment that I was going to do something productive to get my thoughts focused, but I was overwhelmed with exhaustion in the face of doing anything as soon as I reached my bed. It just looked too tempting. Max hopped on to the covers in front of me, padding his paws and glancing up at me with what was clearly a "care to join me?" expression on his face. And yes. Yes, I did.

I crawled back under the covers, staring at the ceiling, and pulled them up to my chin. I hadn't done much of anything today, and I was already exhausted. I knew this was bad, but the allure of getting out of my head for a while was too seductive to turn down, and I found my eyes drifting shut once more.

I woke with a start a few hours later, whipped from the depths of a dream by what I thought was my alarm clock going off, but that I soon figured out was my phone ringing. I pulled myself to my feet, bleary, and tugged the covers around myself as I staggered back to the kitchen. I frowned at the number flashing on the screen and picked it up without thinking. As soon as I lifted it to my ear, my heart dropped as I recalled who I'd been expecting a call from for all this time.

"Edie?"

"Dominic, whose phone are you calling on?" I demanded at once.

"Mine," he replied, sounding confused, and I remembered that I had deleted his number from my cell a few days after I left my job. Shit. My bad.

"Fine," I sighed, my patience already short. "What do you want?"

"I just want to talk," he began, and then he took a deep breath like he was rallying up for a speech—a speech that I had no interest in hearing. I had had enough men monologing at me to last me a lifetime.

"Dominic, I already got a call from Katie."

"Who?"

"Are you fucking kidding me?" I rolled my eyes skyward. "The lead singer of the band. You know, the one that you suddenly changed your mind on?"

"I didn't change my mind on them," he replied, defensively. "It's just that their live shows—"

"That you never went to," I reminded him. I was acting childish but it was so, so satisfying after the way he'd treated me.

"Yeah, I get it," he snapped, a flare of irritation in his voice. He swiftly soothed it, taking a deep breath and then forcing himself to continue.

"So, you know they want you back at the label if they're going to work with us?"

"Yeah, I do," I said, flexing my toes against the cool vinyl of my kitchen floor. "She told me that was how it was."

"Look, I know I fucked up," he sighed deeply, as though he'd been coerced into giving this apology. "But I just need you to…just think about what you're walking away from here. The chance to work with this band. They're going to be big, and you already kind of had them as a pet project—"

"Yeah, but I'm not walking away from anything," I pointed out. "They're walking away from you. And I don't see how that's my problem."

"Don't you want them to succeed?" He implored me. I tightened my lips and let out a sharp breath through my nose; it would be so much more satisfying to let him talk himself into a dumbass corner than to scream at him outright. Slow burn, Edie, slow burn.

"Yeah, I do," I replied. "And I don't think they're going to succeed with a guy who clearly doesn't rate them and, I'd put good money on this, hasn't even listened to their EP yet."

"I'm going to," he protested. "I've just been busy, with them making all these demands—"

"It's not really a ridiculous demand that they want someone who actually likes their music working on their album, Dominic," I shot back, enjoying the way his name felt in my mouth, the way I could spit it out like I'd wanted to so many times when he'd sat there with his brows knitted together waiting for me to finish talking so he could tell me the myriad ways in which I didn't even know I was wrong.

"Look, I don't want to have this debate with you over the phone," he replied, terse. "Can we meet up in person?"

"So that you can try and stick your tongue down my throat again? I don't think so," I replied, feeling that weird, airy, out-of-body feeling that was righteous rage given motion.

"You know I never would have done that if I thought you didn't want it," he protested weakly.

"But you didn't think for a second that you should take a minute and check in with me first?" I pointed out. "If you're so hung up on me being into it."

"That would have ruined the moment," he threw back. "What, am I just meant to get you to sign a fucking contract before I lay a hand on you?"

"Oh, yeah, I forget all the men who get in trouble for not getting fucking written consent before they stick their hands down a girl's pants," I snapped. "You didn't have to get a contract, for fuck's sake, but you could have stopped to ask."

"I just kissed you," he pointed out. "Why is this a big deal?"

"Because I didn't want you to," I replied, voice hard. "And because you didn't take responsibility for any of it."

"What, do I have to apologize now for misreading signals?"

"Yep," I snarled back. "When you take it to HR and make like I'm the crazy one, you have to apologize. We could have worked this out between us, you know that? We could have figured something out. But I'm glad you decided to be a complete fucking jackoff about it, because the thought of spending another minute in that office with you makes me want to take my skin off."

"You're overreacting," he replied bluntly, almost petulant.

"Why does it matter how I'm reacting? We have nothing to do with each other anymore," I pointed out, triumphant. He was making it so easy to stick to my guns and ignore the nagging feeling in my chest that I was passing up a golden opportunity to get back in to a job that I'd worked for so long.

"So, you're not coming back?"

"Dominic, you haven't so much as said 'sorry' to me, do you know that?" I pointed out. "Not once. You don't give a shit about how I feel, you just want to get your way."

"I just don't understand how you feel," he replied, and for a second, I could hear the exasperation in his voice, that brief moment where it clicked that he seriously couldn't see why I would be so upset about this. And I opened my mouth, and I really did intend to tell him everything—to drag him through everything that had led me to that reaction, to the place it had put me in, to how much I wanted to scream at him even now that I knew he would never so much as be in the same building with me again.

But I didn't. Because if he couldn't figure out now what had upset me, then he didn't deserve an explanation. He had tried to feel me up, stuck his tongue down my throat, and then managed to twist it around so that it had become my fault. The thought of dragging myself through all that again just to listen to his pointedly incredulous tone at the other end of the line when it was done—I couldn't. I just couldn't.

"Well, that sucks," I snapped, and hung up the phone. My heart was beating fast in my chest and my cell slid out of my hand and skittered across the surface of the breakfast bar, like I couldn't even bear to have his voice close to me again. The phone started buzzing again at once but I ignored it. I had already made my decision and I wasn't going to back down on it just because he was throwing a tantrum on the other side of the line.

I closed my eyes; it was late in the day now, and Philip was busy tonight so I couldn't even call him up and ask for some guidance on what the hell I should do about this situation. Well, not guidance, but assurance that I hadn't just ruined my career over some petty grudge.

No. Not some petty grudge. I knew I couldn't be in a room alone with Dominic again. I would never stop wondering if what he said to me was meant as a double entendre, if he was reading signals I wasn't sending as my changed mind. I couldn't trust him. That was good enough reason to turn him down. Still, I felt frustrated tears prick my eyes, and I quickly dashed them away with the back of my hand, irritated with myself. Why did I let him get to me like?

I sighed, got to my feet, and pressed the heels of my hands against my closed eyes like I was trying to keep my thoughts from spilling over. I needed to talk to someone, and Max had made it pretty clear that he wasn't interested in stepping in as a furry therapist. No, I needed someone I knew would be on my side till the day I died. Someone who got the industry and knew the position I found myself in right now. I grabbed my phone once it was done ringing again, and quickly called Jeannie before Dominic could start blowing up my phone again.

"What's up?" she asked. She had answered after a couple of rings, yawning loudly into my ear as she spoke. I couldn't help but grin at the sound of her voice.

"Some shit," I groaned. "You want to come 'round to my place? I'll make popcorn or something."

"Popcorn? That good, huh?"

"Oh, it's good," I promised. "And I could use some advice."

"You know how much I love giving my opinion," Jeannie grinned. "I'll be there in an hour?"

"Good, be prepared for a mess."

"I hope you'll get it looking nice and garbage-y specially for me."

"I'll do my best. See you in a bit."

"See you!"

I hung up and instantly felt better; since I had quit my job it had been way too easy to retreat back into this little pit of apathy and antisocial ugliness, especially when I could dress it up under the guise of new relationship nesting. But I was already looking forward to seeing Jeannie, and I knew she wouldn't fuck me around on whether or not I'd just made a seriously dumb decision.

She arrived an hour and ten minutes later, as she tended to do; I had months ago given up on showing up to meetings with Jeannie on time. I would have to just sit there for ten minutes staring at the clock on my phone and wondering if she'd been hit by a truck and whether or not I'd be culpable for it if she had. She waltzed through the door, dropping a kiss on Max's head and handing me a bottle of non-alcoholic sparkling wine.

"You really didn't need to bring this," I said as I took the bottle from her.

"Oh, I did, it's been sitting in my pantry since my aunt came to visit a few months ago and didn't want to drink it with me," she said, and pulled a face. "I need to get rid of it because whipping out the non-alcoholic booze wasn't exactly helping with my romantic life."

"Stop, your compassion is making me swoon," I replied, cocking an eyebrow, but she was already into the kitchen with her hand wrist-deep in the giant bowl of popcorn that I had made for the two of us.

"So, what happened?" she asked through a mouthful of popcorn. I took a deep breath, grabbed a couple of glasses for us, and launched into the whole story. Jeannie gulped down most of the glass of non-wine I'd given her in one fell swoop, cleared her throat, and replied once I was all done.

"That's fucking amazing," she announced and I furrowed my brow at her.

"What do you mean?"

"I mean, you've been given the opportunity of a lifetime," she spread her arms wide like a motivational speaker trying to flog their twelve-step program to success. "This band, you said they're getting big?"

"Yeah, they're doing pretty well," I conceded, even though I knew that was an understatement. It wouldn't be long before they got bored of waiting for me to give an answer and signed with someone else, and that would be the last I heard of them.

"And they want to work with you?"

"Yeah, they want to work with me," I nodded again. "But unless I'm back with the label—"

"Start your own label," she said as she grabbed my hand excitedly. "Oh my God, you'd be so good at it. And you've got a ready-made first band!"

"Jeannie, that's fucking ridiculous," I said, shaking my head and reaching for my glass, more out of instinct than a desire to drink. "Are you sure this shit doesn't have alcohol in it? Because you're talking pretty drunk right now."

"I had eleven shots on the ride over here, but that's beside the point," she joked in that quickfire way she had when she was on to something exciting. "I'm serious, Edie. You don't want to go back and work with Dominic, you haven't got any other job prospects right now—"

"Thanks for reminding me," I muttered. Jeannie waved her hand, quieting me without acknowledgement.

"Seriously, you just need enough cash to book some studio time and you could get them on the map," she went on. "And then you could sign my band, too."

"Oh, I see why you're into this idea all of a sudden," I teased. "Maybe come at it a little more subtlety next time, yeah?"

"Do you have enough in savings to do it?"

"Yeah, just; it'll take away some of my cushion, but—"

"Then I don't see what you're arguing with me for," she cut me off once more. This was the Jeannie I loved and hated the most—the one who would get hardcore hooked on an idea and refuse to let me forget it until I'd given her a damn convincing reason to. And right now, I couldn't come up with one off the top of my head.

"It's not that easy," I muttered. "If it was—"

"You know that it's not as hard as all that," she pointed out again. And she was right—I just needed to file the copyright on my name, figure out my business model, and put in the time to get it off the ground. I had often daydreamed about starting something on my own when I was working with Dominic, but it had always seemed so far off. Partly because he was always convincing me that my taste in music wasn't as attuned as I thought it was, but partly because it was fucking terrifying. Throwing myself out there, especially when I knew I could lose my life savings and look like a total idiot in the process, wasn't the most enticing prospect.

"I don't think they would even want to work with me if it was just me at the label," I countered. "When I was working with Dominic, we had access to a hell of a lot more—"

"You really think those people you worked with are all going to cut you out just because you're not in the office every day? Edie, I know you. People *like* you. And if you frame this as getting one over on Dominic as well, I bet people will be queuing up to help you get this off the ground."

"You sound more excited about this than I do," I said as she paced back and forth over the six feet of clear floorspace that made up my kitchen. "You just want me to sign you, don't you?"

"I'm not going to pretend like I wouldn't totally twist your arm," she flashed me a smile. "But I really think you should do it. You were always complaining that Dominic and the rest of the label stuck with really generic music, right?"

"Yeah, I swear we would just get the same album at least four times a week," I sighed. "But they always seemed to snap it up."

"Then shake up the system!" She threw her hands in the air again, bumping the bowl of popcorn and sending a few kernels flying to the floor. Max darted in to munch them up, eating them too quickly to realize that they weren't cat treats.

"I don't think I'm going to make the music industry give a shit about the music I like overnight," I said, shaking my head at her. I knew I was being a downer, but it wasn't her career on the line here. Surely she knew that she was being at least a little bit ridiculous.

"I think you should do it," she replied firmly, as though that was the end of it. Max coughed up a kernel and glanced up at me angrily, as though I'd tricked him into eating it. I looked between them, grinning, and shook my head.

"You two," I sighed, and then reached for my glass. "I appreciate the vote of confidence but I think I'll need some time to think this one over."

"When you do set it up, let me know," she replied nonchalantly. "I want at least half of the credit."

"At least?"

"At least."

I grabbed a handful of popcorn, hoping it would punctuate the end of this conversation for now, and turned our attention on to other things.

"So, how's the new girlfriend doing?"

"Oh, Reno?" She perked up, and a dirty flicker passed across her face.

"The very same."

"Things are…good," she said slowly. "Really good, actually."

"So, you'll be giving her the keys to your apartment…?"

"Oh, look at you, all hip with the lesbian stereotypes," she bumped my arm with her first. "And that joke is, what, only fifteen years out of date?"

"Come on, fill me in," I looped my hands in the air in front of her, as though drawing the gossip out of her. "I want to hear some good news for a change."

We spent the rest of the night together, Jeannie calling a taxi well past midnight and long after we'd finished an entire cinema's worth of popcorn. We mostly talked shit, ripping the piss out of each other at every chance we got and catching up on all the minutiae of gossip that had been circling around our social group since we'd last seen each other. But the whole time, I couldn't get what she'd suggested out of my head: a record label. My own label. It was a lot. But…

It was true that I had wanted to be further along in my career than I was at that very moment. So maybe I shouldn't wait for someone else to give me the boost up the ladder I was holding out for; maybe I should just get to it myself.

I picked up my phone and saw a text from Philip waiting for me, and smiled as I opened it up. Even being reminded of his existence was enough to pick me up. It was just a simple little goodnight message, nothing special, but I couldn't remember the last time I had dated someone who had given enough of a crap to think of me like that when I wasn't right in front of them. I texted one back, turned over, closed my eyes, and tried to ignore Max pawing at the pillow next to my head. The flicker of a smile played at the corner of my mouth, and for that moment, everything seemed to crystallize in perfect clarity in front of my eyes.

Chapter Sixteen

A week and a therapy session later, I was feeling a little more grounded about everything. Jeannie had helped, and Philip had all but cured me, but I was glad to have a therapist to vent to about everything. She was someone who didn't just hear my opinions, but explained why I might have them and why it was logical for me to stick with them. Every time I walked out of her office I felt a little lighter, and this particular day, as I made my way down those stairs and out into the street, I felt as though I was walking on marshmallow.

I let myself grin when I saw the flurry of red leaves on the tree outside the building; for such a long time, I had done my best to clamp down on anything close to outward displays of emotion. Every time I choked up at something sweet or grinned at something pretty, I found myself irritated by my inability to keep myself under wraps. But, as I distanced myself from The Thing and moved closer to whatever the next big defining moment in my life would be, I found myself more willing to express myself. I had cried at a video of a deer learning to walk two days before and it felt fucking amazing, even if Max was concerned to see me so apparently upset. I felt as though I was easing the pressure on a stuck tap, letting out the feelings I'd kept locked up tight inside since all this had started. Well, now they were coming out, and I was letting myself grin at pretty trees like a character in a vapid romcom. The world could deal with it.

It was one of those crisp, clear, cold mornings, the kind that felt like a clean slate—the air felt sharp in my lungs and my breath formed puffs of steam as it came out of my mouth. I felt like I was blowing smoke, like I had a fire lit somewhere inside of me. That's when I got the second call from Katie.

"Hello?" I paused in the street, ignoring the couple of people who shot me funny looks as they were forced to step around me.

"Hey," she greeted me, sounding a little harassed. "I just wanted to follow up on the call I made last week?"

"Katie, I don't work for the label anymore," I reminded her. "You don't have to be so business-like with me."

"Sorry, sorry," she replied, her voice dropping out of formal. "I've just been dealing with so many businesses in the last week, it's hard to remember that people exist outside their jobs."

She paused for a moment, and I waited for her to put the pieces together.

"So, am I right to assume that you turned down the position at the label?" she asked, and I sighed.

"I'm really sorry I won't be able to work with you there, but I can't go back to work alongside him again," I replied.

"No, I get it." She sighed heavily. "We want to work with the label but I guess I was hoping you could…mitigate him. Dominic is kind of a lot to deal with, especially when he's the one—"

"When he's the one dictating how things are going to be?" I filled in the blanks. "Yeah, trust me, I understand. He's an asshole. And I'm allowed to say that so you don't have to."

"Yeah, he is," she agreed, a gleefully subversive delight showing in her voice, like she was a kid saying "fuck" for the first time. Then she fell silent again.

"I just wanted to say, though, thank you for pushing for us so hard."

There was a sincerity to her tone that I didn't often find working in this business, and I felt a pang of sadness; if things hadn't gone down the way they had maybe we could have been working together. It would have been fun, too—I could have taken them under my wing and guided them through all the ridiculous hoops they'd have to jump through in order to make a splash in an already overcrowded scene. We could have sat around drinking wine and bitching about Dominic. It could have been fun.

Jeannie's words pulsed around my head again, from that night a week ago when she'd come around to talk me through all the bullshit that was going down with the band and Dominic and my old job. I had gone to bed that night unable to shake what she'd said: starting my own label seemed at once so obvious and so impossible that I'd done my best since then to push the oxymoronic thought to the back of my head. But speaking to Katie, knowing how well we would have worked together and the kind of guidance I could have given her through this industry—it flooded back, punching its way to the front of my head and standing there with its hands on its hips. I couldn't ignore it. I had to take the chance.

"Katie," I said, blurting her name out before I could think about the implications of what I was doing. "Could we meet for a coffee? Soon?"

"How soon?" she sounded confused.

"Before you make any big decisions about where you're going to end up," I replied urgently, like she might have a pen hovering over a contract as we spoke. "Could you manage that?"

"How about tomorrow? I'll text you the name of my local place?"

"Yes. Sounds great," I said. "See you then."

I hung up the phone before I could let anything else tumble out of my mouth, and stood there for another moment as I tried to figure out what the hell I thought I was doing. Then I noticed the time and realized that if I didn't hurry up I was going to be late for meeting Philip. I tightened my coat around my shoulders and picked up the pace, already trying to work out how I should tell him what I had just done.

I walked into the little café that he had insisted we give a try to and felt my muscles unclench as the warmer air swept around me. That was better. Philip had this eye for places that I would have dismissed as way too hipster for someone like me, but he always had this firm earnestness about them that kept me from getting too cynical. Well, that, and the fact that he always got cake at the end of the meal and always shared a couple of bites with me. It was hard to roll your eyes about pretentiousness when you had a mouthful of cake to contend with.

I scanned the room, and saw him sitting at a quaint little two-person table in a nook at the far end of the room. He was wearing a thick grey sweater and a pair of heavy rimmed glasses and looked like the librarian I would have crushed on all the way through high school; I glanced down at my jeans and t-shirt and hoped that I could get by on low-maintenance chic.

He waved and I waggled my fingers in return and headed over to join him. He stood up and kissed me on the corner of my mouth, his comforting scent enveloping me.

For a moment, I forgot about labels and bands and jobs and Dominics and my brain was rendered briefly and blissfully clear, but as soon as he pulled away it all came flooding back again.

"Hey," he said as he grinned at me; then he seemed to sense something was wrong and asked, "What's up?"

"I think I've either just done something really smart or really, really stupid," I said. I grimaced and then managed a smile, and he leaned back in his seat and gestured for me to go on.

"Tell me more."

"You remember what I told you that Jeannie was saying, about starting my own label?" I began, and he nodded—it had been four months since we'd really officially met and started dating, and one of the best things about that was not having to qualify every mention of my friends with a reminder of who they were.

"Yes, the thing about starting your own label," he confirmed, a smile curling up on the corners of his mouth. He had been all for it when I'd told him what Jeannie had suggested, but back then I had thought it was easy for them to say that when they weren't the ones putting their careers and maybe even their own reputations on the line. But now, the glimmer in their eyes seemed more like backup than a challenge.

"Yeah, that thing," I said. "I spoke to Jeannie about it and I called up Irina as well and they both told me I should go for it, but I thought it was—I don't know, I thought it was a crazy idea."

"I think it's a decent idea," he replied, with that calming confidence he had that just blamed the panicky parts of my brain.

"Well," I continued. "I just got a call from Katie asking if I'd decided to come back to the label or not and I told her no, and then I kind of invited her out for a coffee tomorrow afternoon."

"Oh?" He perked up, cocking his head at me. "Are you going to pitch it to her? Ask if she'll come on board?"

"I think I kind of have to now," I said, shaking my head and grinning to myself. "It would look pretty weird if I told her to hold off on signing any contracts till she'd talked to me and then just asked about her Christmas plans."

"Do you think she'll say yes? That she'll work with you?" Philip leaned forward, interested. "I bet she will. She'd be crazy not to."

"She'd be crazier to," I corrected him. "Remember that I'd be starting this from the ground up. They'd be putting a hell of a lot of trust in me when they probably already have a bunch of better options."

"But they're all wide-eyed and hopeful about the world, right?" he asked. He grinned, nudging his knee against mine playfully beneath the table. "You could con them into thinking that signing with you would be the right choice."

"Oh, thanks for the vote of confidence," I said, making like I was insulted by the insinuation. But my voice was a little shaky as I realized the implications of what I had done.

"Hey, you're good," he said. He caught my hand, turning it over and tracing the lines of my palms with his index finger gently; I had once fallen asleep when he'd been doing that to me, and he had used it to calm me down ever since. It didn't assuage my panic completely but it was a good step towards making me at least feel cared for.

"I have no clue what the fuck I'm going to say that won't get me laughed out of the place," I said, shaking my head. "Maybe I should text her and ask for a little more time—"

"No way," he replied firmly, pulling my hand to his face and planting a quick kiss on the back of it before he continued. "You said yourself you can't expect them to wait around for ever. Strike now."

"You make it sound like I'm organizing a tactical invasion," I said, smiling weakly.

"Well, you're swiping them out from under your old job's nose," he pointed out. "That's a little bit of military precision, surely."

"Oh, don't say that, I'll feel bad." I waved my hands at him, as though I could make the words dissipate into the air around me.

"Why would you feel bad?" he asked, frowning. "They're the ones who fucked you over. I don't see why you should feel guilty about getting yours."

"That's the dude in you," I teased. "You guys never feel bad about anything."

"Except not sharing cake with you," he replied, cocking an eyebrow. "Or maybe that's just you making me feel guilty?"

"In my defense," I held my hands up. "Cake."

"Fair point," he replied and glanced down at the menu. "Shall we get something? I'm starving."

We ordered and ate and caught up on the news since the last time we'd seen each other, and I found myself putting everything that had been bugging me to the back of my mind for the time being. The effect Philip had on me was something close to ridiculous; it was that sensation I had when I had taken too much cough syrup as a teenager trying to cure my flu before prom, and I had lain there on the bed feeling as though I was sinking into the sheets, the world warm and welcoming as it tightened in around me. That was how it felt being near him; the world seemed smaller and safer than it ever had before. After The Thing had happened, I had truly believed that I would never find a man I could fully trust again, not without doubting myself or second-guessing my interpretation of him or wondering if somewhere, somehow, he could pull something similar to what Kieran had done to me. But when I looked at Philip, I felt this warmth blossoming within me, like he had put down roots inside me.

We finished our food and sat there after splitting the bill, lingering longer than we should have. I had to meet Katie at some point tomorrow and should really be working on my pitch to her. But the real world existed only outside this café and I didn't want to face it quite yet. Not when I could just sit here and debate the merits of first albums with Philip for another hour and a half.

"I should really be getting home," he said, looking down at his watch with a small sigh. He pushed his glasses up his nose and looked at me hopefully, expectantly

"You should come back to mine," I replied firmly. "You've got your laptop with you, right?"

"Right," he grinned. "And besides, you'll need someone to babysit Max while you're at your meeting tomorrow. It would be irresponsible of me not to come over."

"You know, I didn't even think of that." I nodded faux-gravely. "You know how much he definitely notices when I'm out of the house for more than three hours."

"He does," Philip replied, a flicker of a smile playing at the corner of his mouth. "What kind of boyfriend would I be if I didn't step in to comfort him?"

"Boyfriend," I repeated. I shook my head, the word still feeling odd on my tongue. "I still can't get used to that."

"What would you prefer? 'Gentleman caller'?"

"No, because I'm not my mom and I'm not reading a Regency romance novel," I said, rolling my eyes playfully. "It's just been a…a long time since I had anyone I actually wanted to refer to as my boyfriend."

"I'm glad I made the cut," he said. He took my hand and squeezed it and I suddenly felt as though a wellspring had been uncorked inside of me, emotion roiling up dangerously and threatening to make me look like a complete idiot in front of Philip. In the softness in his eyes, especially by the light of the candle that the waitress had insisted on lighting an hour ago, I felt the roots inside me spreading and deepening, the earth shifting to make way for them. I suddenly felt a lump in my throat and glanced away.

"Are you alright?" he asked. He furrowed his brow at me and I nodded.

"I'm great," I replied quickly. "And hey, I'm not the one calling you my boyfriend. That's just you. So, don't get too cocky."

"Oh, I'll bear that in mind," he replied, like I was pitching him a new business venture. "I'm hoping that my commitment to annoying your cat while you're out is enough to get me bumped up to the top spot."

"There's a lot of competition," I warned.

"Oh, is there?"

"Nah, just you," I replied. "And I'm glad I have you."

"Me too," he said. He squeezed my hand again, and I felt the banks holding back my emotionality threaten to burst. *Fuck it.* What was it I had been thinking today, when I had come out of the therapist's office? That I should let myself feel things? Well, some part of me really, really wanted to feel this, and I was going to let it happen. I opened my mouth and tried not to let that cloying, teenage-girl part of my brain put a stop to me.

"I know this hasn't been…I know it hasn't been perfect," I admitted haltingly. "And I…you've stuck around through so much. You came into my life when things were so fucking nightmarishly difficult and sometimes it felt like they just got harder from then on and you, you're still here.

You never let any of that faze you. You're just…good. I don't meet a lot of good people, Philip, but you're just…good."

The word felt so inadequate, the sort of thing my high school English teacher would have scolded me for putting in a sentence instead of something more expressive, but in that moment, that's the only thing that could truly sum up how I felt about him. His goodness radiated out from him, past those nerdy sweaters and the thick glasses, and lit up the corners of my life that had felt midnight-black.

"I love you."

It took me a second to realize that it was me saying those words. It was one of those odd, out-of-body, cough-syrup moments once more, and it wasn't until I saw the surprise on Philip's face that I figured out that, yeah, that had been me.

"I love you too," he replied after a moment's pause, and a grin that I was surprised even fit in the damn restaurant spread across his face. I found mine mirroring his, and the two of us let out nervous little laughs, as though we couldn't quite believe that we'd both said that.

"I haven't said that to anyone in a long time," he admitted.

"I haven't meant it like that in a long time," I replied. "But…I love you. A lot."

"I love you too," he repeated, and I felt my heart tingle in my chest. For a moment, it felt like I'd been inflated, like I was going to float away from the table under the power of the words he'd just said to me. But I stayed in my seat, and found my mind drifting towards more earthly pursuits.

"Come on, let's get back to my place," I suggested, and I could tell from the look in his eyes that he knew precisely what I was suggesting.

"Taxi, or walk?"

"Oh, we don't have time to walk." I shot a look over my shoulder at him as we both got to our feet.

It didn't take us long to find a cab, and soon enough we were back at my apartment; Philip kissed the back of my neck as I went to unlock the door, and I paused for a moment, snuggling back against him.

"Come on, come on," he said, hurrying me along playfully as he slid his hands around my waist from behind. "I can't wait all night, you know."

"Right, of course," I mumbled, remembering myself. I unlocked the door and the two of us tumbled over the threshold, just like we had done that first night when I had brought him back here and things hadn't ended as well as I'd hoped they would. This time, though, things felt different, and as I turned to pull him against him, an uptick of excitement fluttered in my chest. It was going to happen tonight. Just you watch. Or don't, because that would be kind of gross.

Our mouths met hungrily and he wrapped himself around me, drawing my body close against his; I could feel his cock already growing hard against my leg, and the two of us stumbled back a few feet to lean against the table so I could wrap my leg around him and grind against him. My pussy was already slick with needing him, with knowing what was coming next, and my skin seemed to hold his fingerprints at every spot he touched me. I was ready for this. Ready for more.

"Bedroom?" he asked, and much as I was tempted to suggest that we go for it right there in the kitchen, the disinfecting job I'd have to do wasn't quite as attractive.

"Bedroom," I replied breathlessly and, to my surprise, he scooped me up in his arms and carried me all of the way to the bed. I giggled and wrapped my arms around his neck, brushing my lips against his ear in that way that I knew he loved, and he laid me down on top of the covers. Max, who had been asleep on the pillow, sprung to wakefulness and hurried away to the living room.

"Oops, sorry, baby," I muttered after him, but I hardly had time to feel bad for my little kitten before Philip was on top of me once again. I slipped my hand beneath his sweater, the scratchy fabric warm against my skin, and felt the flex of his spine beneath my fingers. Fuck, he felt good. He always did.

It was a cold night, and by the time we had both stripped down we had to slide beneath the covers to keep warm. His hands reached for me beneath the sheets, and his warm fingers on my cold skin felt even better than usual. There was something both intensely hot and oddly chaste about making out with him like this, when I could feel every contour and muscle in his body flush against mine but his hands were staying firmly above the waist. I hooked my leg over his and drew him closer, his cock nudging up against my clit and making me sigh with pleasure.

"You feel so good tonight," he murmured into my ear before letting his mouth trail down me. I knew what he meant; I had lost count of all the times I had craved his touch like this, but tonight something felt different. It was like there was a pull deep in my belly towards him, like I wanted to slip inside his skin. On that cold night, the movement of our bodies against each other felt like the ebb and flow of the tide and I couldn't get enough of it.

I took his hand and pulled it between my legs; I was wet already and needed some relief, and didn't have the words to ask for it. He turned his hand around and stroked my clit gently with two fingers, easing me into the pressure—but that wasn't what I wanted, no matter how good it felt. No, I caught his hand and pulled it further down, until his fingers were against my slit.

"You sure?" he murmured, his lips brushing up against mine as he spoke. I nodded.

"I'm sure," I assured him softly, and he slowly began to push one finger inside of me. He moved slow but it still hurt a little, a pinching sensation deep inside me. I breathed deep, letting the air stretch the skin across my stomach, and felt something give—something relaxing as he moved his finger into me, and then added another. I winced, but it was more from instinct than from any kind of specific pain.

"You okay?"

"Yeah, yeah," I assured him, leaning up and kissing him again, focusing on the feel of his lips against mine as I finally, finally began to relax around him. It still hurt a little, but it felt more like it did when I lost my virginity than anything else—a pain that led to the promise of something more, instead of an unassailable stop sign in my sex life.

I hooked one leg over him, allowing him better access, and pressed my forehead to his chest, focused on the sound of his heartbeat steady in his chest. He began to fuck me with his fingers, taking his time, and I reached down with my hand so I could caress my clit at the same time; fuck, that felt good. And then it hit me—that felt *good*. It didn't hurt, it wasn't even the kind of neutral, numb lack of sensation that I could get used to. It actually felt *good*.

I reached between his legs with my other hand and felt for him, wrapping my fingers around his cock, and realized that I could imagine how good it would feel to have him inside me. I wanted to feel him in me. I started to stroke his cock, and felt his heartbeat pick up pace against my skin. There was something so intimate about it, hearing his heart like that, the thrum of blood in his veins. I moved my fingers against my clit with more purpose and he slowly pushed another finger inside of me, spreading me, better than any one of those stupid dilators sitting my drawer a few feet away.

"Can we...?" I asked. I knew that he was more than a little skittish after the last few times we'd tried had gone so wrong, but surely he had to see that this was better than usual. We had to try. It felt strange to be thinking of consummating the relationship after we'd exchanged "I love yous", but there was something sweet about it in a teenage-romance kind of way. Like we had been saving ourselves. And I guess that, in some ways, my body had made that decision for me even if I hadn't been on board.

"We can try," he murmured in response, tipping my head up so I could look at him. There was a nervousness in his gaze that I was sure was reflected in mine, but a certainty, too. I flipped over, reached for a condom out of the drawer, and pressed it into his hand. I ran my hand lightly across his chest as he sheathed himself, and he leaned over to kiss me once more before he pulled me on top of him. I placed my hands on his shoulders to steady myself, and felt a twitch of panic in my chest that I did my best to ignore. *If it didn't work, it didn't work.* I still loved him and he still loved me. I didn't have to do this because I was scared of him leaving without it; I was doing it because I wanted him. I wanted this.

I reached down and wrapped my fingers around him, holding him steady, and he gripped my hips to guide me down. I went slow at first—so slow that for a moment I wasn't sure anything was happening at all, but I felt a small, sharp shock of pain as he entered me for the first time. I flinched and he stopped at once, though I could see the tension in his jaw, the need in his eyes.

"Are you okay?"

"I'm fine," I said determinedly. I should have known that it wasn't going to be as easy as true love curing all, but that hadn't kept me from hoping. Still, I closed my eyes, pressed my lips together, and kept moving—and to my shock, I took him. One inch, two inches, three inches, and before I knew it he was all the way inside of me. I held him there for a long moment, savouring the feeling, letting myself get used to it. It had been so long since someone had been inside me like this, and I couldn't help but remember the last time—how ugly it had been, how I had been sure it had ruined me, how I had been certain that even if I could physically do this, I would never find it in me to want to again. But I did. I could. Philip didn't take his eyes from mine, his gaze unblinking, as though he was worried that he might shatter the moment if he so much as made a move. But I smiled down at him and he let his eyes fall shut for a moment.

"Fuck, you feel so good," he gasped, as though he'd been holding in a breath all this time—not just since he had entered me, but since the moment we'd met, since the start of it all. I knew how he felt. After all that time and all that energy put into trying to make myself right again, I was finally blurring out the edge of those bad memories with new ones.

We fucked, and it felt good. It was a sentence so simple that I would have rolled my eyes if it turned up in one of the erotic fanfiction stories I had read as a teenager, but to me, right then, it was a revelation. After struggling so long with so much pain, I could just…do it. Yes, there were still flickers of discomfort now and then, moments when I had to slow or steady him, but we did it. And it felt *good.*

After a while he sat up and slipped his arms around me, pressing his head into my shoulder and grinding up and into me. I gripped his hair and pulled it back so I could kiss him again, and our tongues met and seemed to move in time with his thrusts, and all of a sudden, the feeling swelled over me.

"Jesus," I panted against his mouth, the orgasm building and cresting so quickly that it made my vision blur around the edges. My pussy clenched around his cock and with every pulse the pleasure grew, radiating out and warming my skin from the inside out.

"Fuck..." Philip breathed against my ear, sliding his hand up my back and cradling my head, drawing me close so all I could feel was his skin against mine. And then, with a sharp breath out against my skin, he came, his cock twitching inside of me a couple of times while he held himself deep in my pussy.

I wasn't sure how long we stayed there, arms wrapped around each other, like we were waiting to float back down to Earth. It took a while, my head still spinning from the unfamiliar intensity of what had just happened. It had been so long that I had almost forgotten how good it felt to fuck like this. Everything else had been good, but this was different. More intense. Maybe it was the "I-love-yous" before, or maybe it was just that it had been so long, but I sort of felt like I had lost my virginity all over again. Except this time, it hadn't been in a tent at someone's graduation party and I had actually enjoyed it.

Eventually, he slowly withdrew from me, and I winced as he pulled himself out.

"Are you okay? Does it hurt?" He asked, stroking my hair back from my face and looking intently into my eyes. I grinned and shook my head.

"No, I just...it's like relearning everything, that's all," I explained as best I could. "All of this feels new."

"Hey, I haven't had sex for at least as long as you have," he pointed out. "I'd like to think I'm not that much out of touch."

"Yeah, but you know it's different for me," I pointed out, letting out a yawn. I'd forgotten how it felt to be sated deep down in my soul; not that I hadn't been satisfied by everything we'd been doing up till now. But now that I had finally managed it again and now that the weight had lifted from my shoulders, I was aware of just how much it had been getting under my skin the last few months.

"I know," he said, planting a kiss on my forehead. "Is it weird to say I'm proud of you?"

"It would be a little bit, yeah," I teased. "I don't want you to sound like my little league coach right after you've been inside me."

"I'll accept that," he replied seriously. "Do you think you know what changed? I mean, tonight compared to everything else that…you know, every other time we tried."

"I don't know," I shrugged. "I guess it could have been…I mean, it could have been that we finally did the whole 'I love you' thing…"

"You really think that might have had something to do with it?" He screwed up his face.

"Why wouldn't it have?"

"It just seems a little convenient," he said, cocking an eyebrow. "I don't think your vagina suddenly snapped back open because it figured out that I was actually committed to you."

"True love's pussy," I giggled. "I guess you're right, it sounds a little absurd when you put it like that."

"I'm just glad we finally got there," he lay down, staring at the ceiling and reaching out to me. I slipped down next to him, flopping my arm out across his chest. I could still feel his heartbeat, thrumming, permanent.

"Me too," I sighed, as he ran his fingers through my hair idly, sending a shiver down my spine.

"So, what now?" he asked. "We did the 'I love yous' and the first time having sex tonight. I don't know what other firsts I can come up with."

"First time going out for breakfast so I can go over my pitch to this woman tomorrow?" I suggested hopefully, and in the dark, I could almost hear him smile.

"Sounds good," he said, as he lifted his head slightly to see Max jumping up on to the covers to join us. He reached out a hand and my cat came scrabbling over to him, bouncing joyfully up on his chest like his entire face was made of cheese and the tuna I had earmarked for breakfast. I watched the two of them as Max aggressively bumped his head into Philip's chin, and I grinned. It was one of those tiny moments that instantly engraved itself on to my memory, every detail—the feel of his heartbeat, the warmth of his skin, the way Max's tail flopped against my face for a couple of seconds before he settled down. I screwed my nose up to get his fluff off me, and let my head flop down on to the pillow. It had happened. Finally. All of it.

Chapter Seventeen

I SAT IN THE COFFEE SHOP where I had met Philip for the first time, an event that now felt like a lifetime ago. I should have been peering around the place with a slightly smug nostalgia given everything that had been happening with us over the last couple of weeks, but instead I found myself feeling as though my head was going to give out under the stress of what I was currently trying to do.

"You're going to be fine." Philip's words echoed in my head again, and I clung to them like a life raft. I had treated him to breakfast that morning, despite his protestations, and we had sat together in that same diner we'd gone to on our first proper date with our knees bumping under the table, grinning like a pair of teenagers over a double-strawed milkshake. Ever since I had gotten the label off the ground, I had actually been able to pay for shit for a change and it felt like it made all the difference; there was something about letting him cover everything that made me feeling like he was buying me, a sensation I'd always been uncomfortable with. But now I was paying him back in breakfasts and movie tickets and concert trips and I was proud to treat my man.

"I'm just nervous," I'd whined to him earlier that day, glancing down at my watch as though the time might have snuck up on me without me spotting it. "What time did I say I was meeting them again?"

"At six, at the coffee shop, and you know that," he pointed out again gently. "You need to chill. Everything's in hand."

"I know, I know," I sighed, running my fingers through my hair and staring down at my hands. They were shaking slightly, like I'd just given blood.

"It's just the first time," I defended myself. "I'm panicked, that's all. If this goes wrong…"

"Then I suppose you'll just have to go to the bands you signed and let them know that all of this was actually a terrible mistake and that you're very sorry but you're not going to be able to represent them anymore," he replied bluntly, and I grinned. He had a way of making me feel better about even my dumbest insecurities.

"I get it," I conceded, finally taking a bite of my breakfast quesadilla. "Hey, you're still coming tonight, right?"

"Wouldn't miss it," he said, as he grinned and squeezed my hand across the table. I would have smiled back, but I didn't want to spray him with egg and tortilla.

I had suggested meeting in the coffee shop just because it meant that all of us could stay far away from alcohol for the time being, which was something that I didn't need in my life right now. I had had a few drinks here and there over the last month or so—mostly to take the edge off of the stress of starting a label of my own—but the last thing I needed tonight was to get drunk and end up unable to handle whatever inevitable disaster was going to come up now that I'd thought of it. The door chimed, I looked up, and I found myself staring at the band who had gotten my label off the ground in the first place. All three of them were there—keyboardist, drummer, guitarist, my holy trinity.

"Katie, Jenna, Abby," I greeted them. I got to my feet and managed a smile, hoping they couldn't see the sheer panic in my face. "Are you ready for tonight?"

"Hell, yes," Jenna grinned, always the more forward of the three. "Ready for action."

"Are we just heading straight there?" Katie asked, frowning slightly; I saw a lot of myself in Katie, in her nervousness and her inability to let go of the small things. I nodded.

"Straight there," I confirmed. "I just wanted to take you there myself and be certain you weren't going to bail on me."

Katie rolled her eyes, but smiled.

"You really think we're going to fuck you over like that? After all this time?"

"Hey, never trust a musician," I teased. "You ready?"

"Whenever you are."

We headed outside to hail a cab and took it straight to the venue that I'd booked for the night; outside, there was a crowd a good hundred people strong waiting for the doors to open, huddling against the frigid November air.

"Holy shit, there's so many people," Jenna gasped, and I allowed myself a tiny, victorious smirk. I had worked hard on marketing this gig—it was my first big performance, after all, and I wanted it to land—and it looked like it had worked. I knew we had almost sold out on tickets and it looked like there was going to be a fair amount of competition for the ones that remained.

"Come on 'round the back, I don't want you mobbed by your fans," I said. I hustled them in the back entrance, only half-joking; the couple of tracks they'd released a few weeks before, after some hurried time in the studio following signing with my fledgling label, had blown up in a serious way—they were already getting shared hundreds of times across social media. It was vindicating every single time I saw someone talking up their music, a reminder that my ear had been right all along. Every time I found myself doubting myself or wondering what in the name of holy hell I was doing starting my own label, I reminded myself of that. Sometimes, it even helped.

"Hey, Edie!" Jeannie greeted me; she was in full stage regalia, hair teased big and eyes outlined with a stark graphic liner like something off a Bowie album cover. "You alright? You look like you're going to pop."

"I might," I replied hurriedly. "You and Reno doing okay? Ready to go?"

"Of course we are," she beamed. "I'm so excited. I haven't played in—"

"Babe, you know I would listen to you any other time, but I have to run around this place at least three more times and check that everything's how I want it." I put my hand on her shoulder and looked intently into her eyes. "I'll catch you in ten minutes?"

"Go ahead," Jeannie said, waving her hand good-naturedly. "You got me this gig, you can talk to me however you want. Hey, Lena and Irina texted me, they said they're in the crowd tonight and that they're going to try their very best to put me off."

"Don't say that unless you want to bear the full brunt of my stress right now," I warned her, and then I hurried off to make sure everything was in place. Reno and Jeannie had been working on a few songs together since I'd started the label and, while we'd all agreed that me signing them would be the death knell for our friendship, I managed to squeeze them in on a supporting slot at this gig. It wasn't much, but it was a good platform for them to test out their new tracks and besides, I liked what I had heard from them so far. I would have been a fool not to take them up on the offer.

I charged around backstage so fast that I barely had time to take anything in; I had helped out in organizing gigs before but had never had this much personal investment in one, and it fucking *sucked.* Was it going to be like this every time? I felt as though I had been running on nervous energy for the last full week, and it wasn't doing me much good. I felt as though, as Jeannie said, I was going to pop.

And yet, I wouldn't have changed any of this for the world. Ever since I had started Max Recordings—yes, named after my cat, because I'm wildly unoriginal—it felt as though the world had slowly been in the process of righting itself once again. It took its sweet-ass time and sometimes I worried that funnelling the last of my savings into this was going to prove to be the stupidest idea I'd ever come up with, but as it was, things were starting to make sense once more. I wouldn't have changed it. Well, maybe I would have put aside some cash for an assistant, but it was too late for that now and besides, I was an overachiever; I couldn't hand off any of my responsibilities to someone else, or I'd launch into full-blown panic mode at the thought of someone else mucking it up for me.

"Are you guys ready to go?" I had rounded back to Reno and Jeannie, who were holding hands and giggling over something in the corner; any other time and I would have been charmed by their adorableness, but right then I needed them ready to go at a moment's notice. Jeannie glanced up, seemed to read the stress on my face at once, and nodded. She even threw in a little salute that I knew was meant in good fun.

"Whenever you are," she nodded, and my shoulders sagged with relief. I looked down at my watch. It was almost time to kick things off.

"You want us to head out?" Jeannie asked, and I nodded. This was really happening. This was really, actually happening.

"Yeah, I think that the door's been open and everyone's in now." I paused for a moment, straining my ears to make out the hundreds of voices waiting for us to come out and perform already. I felt my chest tighten and my palms starting to sweat, as though I was the one about to walk out on stage and perform for the first time. In some ways, I was. In others, I really wasn't, and I needed to gather everyone together and get them ready to head out.

"Now," I said, squeezing Jeannie's arm again; she leaned in and gave me a quick hug, her musky perfume filling my senses and creating a warm little bubble around me for a moment.

"It's going to be fine," she mumbled in my ear. "You've done brilliantly."

And then, she pulled back and marched out on to the stage. The sound of the crowd swelled and my heartrate increased to near-fatal levels. Okay, it was out of my hands now.

"Edie?" A voice came from behind me, and I turned to find a boy a few years younger than me shooting me a nervous look. "There's a man at reception who says you're waiting for him?"

"Philip? Is that his name?"

The boy nodded.

"Send him in," I said, my pounding heart dropping by a few beats per minute.

"That your boyfriend?" Jenna asked, grinning like she'd caught her teacher canoodling around the back of the schoolyard, and I nodded.

"Sure is," I replied proudly. It was still a little odd to think of him like that, as my boyfriend—it had been weeks since we had first used that term but it still felt like I was making him up, that a man as good as him couldn't possibly really exist. I had even told my mom about him this week, and she had practically swooned off the phone with excitement that I was finally seeing someone again. Of course, she had no idea about everything that had brought me to him, all the struggles we'd had to overcome to get where we were, but it was still sweet that she gave a damn who I was dating (or that I was dating at all).

"Hey!" Philip strode into the backstage area with a big smile on his face. "It's packed out there, I had to practically fight my way in."

"Really?" Katie's eyes widened with excitement, and he nodded.

"Just wait till you see it," he said. Katie glanced over at Jenna, looking as though she might burst on the spot.

"How are you doing?" Philip asked me, scanning my face. "You alright?"

"Uh, sort of trying not to pass out with nervousness but otherwise doing great," I replied, my voice shaky. Philip grinned and pulled me into his arms.

"You're fine, trust me," he assured me. "Everything looks great, and Jeannie and Reno sound good."

"They do, don't they?" I conceded, my ear finally tuning in to what they were playing; it was upbeat, a bop, the kind of thing that had me shuffling my feet without even noticing I was doing it.

"You know everything's going to be alright, don't you?" Philip asked, wrapping his arms around me, holding me still and steady. I closed my eyes, took a deep breath, and planted a quick kiss on the corner of his mouth.

"Yeah, I do," I finally said. Except this time, I actually meant it.

About the Author

Louise MacGregor is an internationally-published writer of fiction, pop culture criticism, and feminist social commentary. A graduate of journalism and history from the University of Stirling, Louise brings her passion for women-centric stories to both her fiction and non-fiction. As well as running the long-standing pop cultural blog *The Cutprice Guignol* and film criticism outlet *No But Listen*, Louise has written boundary-pushing, genre-defying works such as *Ruthless* and *Trouble Clef* under her pen name, Kara Lowndes. Now turning her attention to contemporary feminist social critique, *Right Guy, Wrong Time* is Louise's first full-length novel. She resides in Glasgow, Scotland, with her partner and her cat.